The Christmas Caper
A Love and Larceny Historical Romance
Nan Sampson

Last Chance Press

Acknowledgements

Huge thanks to my family, my dear friends in the Hive, and the crew at Conscious Cup Coffee Roasters in Crystal Lake for enormous support and many cups of excellent tea and coffee. You keep me on the path and ever inspired.

Contents

Chapter 1

Nicola

London

1870

I n and out, like a ghost. That was the plan. Home before the coals in the grate had faded to charcoal gray.

By the light of a late December half-moon, and the dim glow of a streetlamp, Nicola Byrne vaulted the low, wrought-iron fence that surrounded Samuel "Sammy the Smoke" Byrne's London townhouse in Portman's Square, and slipped around the side of the brick structure to the window next to the servant's entrance. She needed neither moonlight nor gas lamp to find her way; she'd grown up in this house and had breezed in and out in her teenage rebellion years to play snooker at her father's club dressed as a boy.

Mrs. Lambeth, the housekeeper, had never locked this particular window, despite, or perhaps because she knew Nick, as her friends called her, used it to get in and out after her parents had gone to bed. But that was ages ago, and now that her uncle had taken over the property, tossing Nick out on her ear after her father's death last year, there was no guarantee the window would still allow her ingress.

Through the thick windowpane, she could see the night candle in its slender hurricane globe glowing on the long trestle table in the kitchen, though the staff would all be in bed at this late hour. And as she'd ascertained that afternoon, the master of the house, her uncle, Samuel Byrne, would be playing cards at the home of one of his nefarious friends until the early hours of the morning.

She rubbed her hands on her men's black trousers. She'd broken into dozens of houses over the past ten years with cool sangfroid. Why did her palms sweat tonight? Pressing against the sash, she pushed up.

The window slid easily, greased in its tracks, and without a sound. God bless Mrs. Lambeth, the only one of the original staff her uncle had kept on.

She scrambled through and dropped lightly to the floor. A pause to listen for any reaction, then she was up the back stairs and down the hall to what had once been her father's study. Her hand hesitated on the knob. She'd been back twice since Sammy the Smoke, as London's underworld knew him, had evicted her from her home. The first time had been the worst. Sam had stripped the room of everything her father had loved, save for one thing. Gone were the dramatic landscapes by Turner and Constable, his small collection of Roman coins and Egyptian ushabtis, two ornate Louis XV jewelry boxes, most of his academic books, and the cubbies of scrolls he'd spent his career translating.

Where Arthur Byrne had chosen a life of teaching and learning upon arriving in London as a young man from County Wicklow, his brother Sam had followed his baser instincts and now ranked as one of the city's most successful extortionists and smugglers. Sam wouldn't know a Turner from a Van Gogh. Whether Sam ordered the objects that Nick's father had treasured trundled off to the attic or discarded them like the rubbish Sam likely thought they were, Nick wasn't sure. But their absence sent a knife of grief and despair slicing through her heart.

The only thing Sam had left was the portrait of Nick's mother, Augusta Newton Byrne, which took pride of place over the mantel. For reasons Nick had never quite understood, Arthur Byrne had worshipped his wife. Unfortunately, so had many others.

The framed canvas had still been there on Nick's second and last visit, when she'd begged her uncle to let her have the painting of her mother.

He'd denied her with a louche sneer. "Artie wasn't the only one who loved Augusta. I was quite fond of her myself."

Bad enough Augusta Byrne had entertained a string of "admirers" throughout her marriage. That one of those lovers might have been Sam made Nick nauseous.

Still. Nick had to have that painting. Not because she wanted her mother's beautiful but traitorous face smiling down with its accustomed smugness from her own parlor fireplace, but because of what her mother had hidden in the lining behind the painting.

She wiped her hands again and eased the shiny brass latch down. She'd half expected the door to be locked. Instead, the latch clicked, and she eased open the heavy oak door a crack, checking for light beyond.

Nothing. No glow from a gas lamp or candle, and the kind of silence that only came from an empty room. That was another thing she'd learned over the last ten years of larceny; how to tell whether a room held an occupant.

She entered and closed the door behind her, scanned the room before taking another step. She knew this room too, in the dark. Sam hadn't rearranged the furniture, and even with the heavy drapes closed over the broad expanse of almost floor-to-ceiling windows, she had no trouble picking her way to the fireplace.

She had just slipped the cylindrical leather blueprint case from her shoulder and pulled a small knife with which to liberate the painting from its heavy gilt frame when she heard the faintest footfall from the hall.

Bloody hell.

Hurrying across the oriental carpet, she slipped behind the waterfall of velvet curtains, something she'd done often growing up as the latch clicked and the door to hall opened.

Chapter 2

Jack

J ack Delacroix slipped into the study and held his breath, listening. He could have sworn he'd heard movement from inside the second after he'd committed himself, but now the room was silent as a tomb.

Which is what it might become if Sammy the Smoke turned out to be in residence instead of playing cards with Eddie Maitland and Max Bernard at The Whistling Pig. However unlikely, Maitland could have lied to Jack. He was a con man, after all, and slick as they come.

Jack scanned the masculine enclave, eyes now well-adjusted to the dark. It looked like every other large, well-appointed gentleman's study, though he didn't think anyone had ever called Sammy the Smoke, the most notorious extortionist and smuggler this side of the Atlantic, a gentleman. A large desk dominated the room, littered with papers, an ashtray full of what smelled like cigar butts, an oil lamp with a pebbled red, milk glass shade, and the remains of a glass of something that might have been whiskey. A comfy chair upholstered in red leather sat waiting for a man with a book. And bookshelves for that man lined three walls and wrapped around a fireplace across from the desk, with the fourth wall taken up by two enormous windows dressed, predictably, in red velvet draperies. All very rococo.

Jack surmised the place had changed little since the house's previous owner, Sammy's stuffy law-abiding brother, who'd been some kind of toff at London City College, died the previous November.

He ignored the bookshelves. He might find a hidden passage behind one, but not the safe he searched for. No, that would likely be near the desk, or...he glanced over at the fireplace and the portrait of a strikingly beautiful woman, likely the professor's lady wife.

Had the old boy been that prosaic? Behind the painting?

Jack crossed to the hearth and tugged at the lower right-hand corner of the frame, hoping it would pull away like a hinged door.

Damn. No luck.

His Aunt Madeleine would have told him nothing was ever that easy. Her younger sister, Matilde, would applaud him for trying the easy solution first. More efficient.

Not that either of the aged grande dames who'd raised him had ever burgled a house. But they had escaped death several times during their harrowing flight from France after the revolution, to hear them tell the tale, picking up skills peculiar to ordinary women of their station.

Or, as he sometimes thought, they were just two dotty old women, living in a fantasy of their own making. Maybe their obsession with Marie Antoinette, to whom they claimed to be related, was nothing more than harmless ravings. Whatever the truth, it didn't matter. They'd taken in a four-year-old Jack after the death of his parents, and while his childhood in that falling-down manor house on the windy Yorkshire moors had been unconventional, he'd been happy, well-cared for, and most importantly, loved.

Which was why he was here to begin with. To keep those two potty old dears in familiar surroundings. To fix the roof, replace a few leaky windows, and make sure he could pay the couple he'd hired from the village to look after them when he wasn't around. Not to mention, he owed Sam Byrne a more personal payback. And while Jack himself wasn't powerful enough to take down the crime lord, any little pain he could cause the snake would help him sleep at night.

If Jack could deprive Sammy the Smoke of what the man said he had, letters from several highly placed members of Parliament professing in turgid terms their affection for Professor Arthur Byrne's wife, it would be Jack who could set his own terms for keeping those letters from the press.

No need to be greedy. A small monthly payment from each of the men would at least keep him and his aunts in beans and onions.

He looked up at the painting again. The safe had to be there. It only made sense. Maybe it opened from the other side?

He reached for the lower left corner—and froze. A faint creak from just outside the door to the study raised the hairs on the back of his neck.

Bloody hell.

The windows? Maybe he could get out that way. Or at least hide in the heavy drapes. He almost laughed. The idea was ridiculous, like some corny drawing room farce.

The click of the latch forced his hand. He raced across the room and slipped behind the curtain of red velvet as the study door opened and someone turned up the gas on the wall sconce, flooding the place with light.

Chapter 3

Nicola

Nick stared in open-mouthed amazement, then anger, as the man slid into her hiding place and froze. His expression must have matched hers, a sort of fishy goggle.

They locked eyes, still as statues and ears pricked, as Sam Byrne clomped across the floor, chatting to someone with him.

"You'll bloody well stay in the hall," groused her uncle. "Don't trust you not to nick something."

Nick glared at the man beside her and mouthed, "You!" She hoped he saw the aggravated exclamation mark in her eyes.

He, being fellow-thief Jack Delacroix, quirked his lips in a smile that gave the impression of being a polite tip of his hat. Probably thought he was charming. He too mouthed, "You," but she sensed no exclamation mark, just an insouciant lift of his black eyebrows over cognac-colored eyes.

Neither could move. Nick barely breathed, not wanting to disturb the heavy curtain in the slightest. But she longed to kick Delacroix hard enough to break bone. He deserved it after that night last May when he'd snagged Lady Beatrice's ruby and diamond necklace just moments before Nick had managed to unlatch the third-story casement to the lady's boudoir. Delacroix had, she learned later, entered the easy way, invited in by the now satiated, sleeping woman.

Her uncle's heavy footsteps brought him closer. He was less than three feet away now.

She heard the desk chair roll across the carpet and then the sound of Sam Byrne's labored breathing as he bent over to access the safe he'd installed behind his desk.

The dial spun, and she felt like she could hear the tumblers clicking. With a thunk, he yanked the door open, and he fumbled around inside before slamming it closed and spinning the dial again. He grunted as he straightened his not inconsiderable bulk.

Thudding footsteps retreated toward the study door, and Nick let out a slow breath. Maybe there was yet a way to salvage this night. If her uncle would just leave, she could still smuggle the painting out.

And what, the obnoxious little voice that lived in her head said, are you going to do about *him*?

Him being Delacroix.

"'ere now," Sam was saying. "Take this, make the payment to Mr. Zhang, then come back after you've stowed those crates in the warehouse."

"Thanks, Boss. Sorry about interruptin' your game."

Byrne's voice slid into his henchman like an icy knife. "Do it again, and it will be your last time doing anything."

"Yes, boss. Sorry, boss. You still got time to go back," the man offered, trying to make amends. Nick felt for him. There was no making amends with Sammy the Smoke. The poor fellow would be feeding the fishes in the Thames by morning. If, that is, the Thames contained any fish left to feed.

"Nah. I got some work to catch up on. But I'll walk you out. Don't trust you wandering around my house by yerself."

The two men exited the study, but her uncle had left the door open. She waited until she heard two sets of footsteps on the carpeted stairs, then turned to the windows. It was the only way to escape now if Sam meant to come back up here.

Delacroix had reached the same conclusion. He watched as she unlatched the casement and then, all gentlemanly, offered his linked hands to boost her up onto the ledge. She ignored him and climbed to the sill, bracing herself as she prepared to make the leap to an ancient, sturdy elm that grew in the back garden.

She felt the tickle of Delacroix's breath on her neck. "Hurry, luv, he's coming back up the stairs."

She considered waiting until she was sure her uncle had discovered Delacroix, but that would delay her own departure, and the chance existed that her competitor would somehow take her down with him. With a frustrated sigh, she made the jump to the branch, catching it with both hands. She propelled herself hand over hand down the sloping branch toward the bole of the tree, then dropped the ten feet to the ground and scrambled aside. She'd no wish for Delacroix to fall on her.

He landed a few feet away with cat-like grace, making her feel like an awkward fawn learning to stand. "Not your first time here, eh? Where now?" He spoke into her ear, and she shivered in response.

She pointed to a line of junipers that lined the fence in the back, where the shadows grew as thick as the berries did in late spring. She sprinted twenty feet, bent low, and slid between two of the towering trees. Delacroix was right behind her.

Not stopping, she pulled herself up and over the top of the wrought-iron fence, taller here than in the front, and landed in a crouch on the cobblestones of the alley behind the row of houses. Her luck held. No one loitered, unless you counted an alley cat that slunk away with a hiss, its sleek back arched in irritation.

She lurked motionless in the shadows as Delacroix landed, silent as that damned cat. In the light of the moon, she could see he was smiling.

"Jolly good fun, eh?" He took in her warm, black, cable knit jumper and the black wool newsboy's cap from which a few errant strands of hair had escaped and cocked his head to one side. "You know, last time we met—and what a memorable night that was, no?—I thought you a young lad. I see now I was mistaken. Very much mistaken. I can only blame the darkness and my unpardonable haste."

He was, she noted, similarly garbed, right down to the black trousers and lace-up boots. Must be what all the fashionable burglars were wearing this season.

She ignored his words. "What are you doing here?"

He yanked off her cap, then his own, and watched as her honey blond hair tumbled down around her shoulders. "I could ask you the same question, but I think we both know the answer." He took her arm as though they were a genteel couple on a late-night stroll and guided her toward an intersecting lane.

When they reached Upper Berkeley Street, Nick stopped and yanked herself free. She puffed out a frustrated breath that hung frosty in the air. "Good night, Mr. Delacroix."

He had the nerve to chuckle. "A pleasure seeing you again also, Miss, uh...I beg your pardon, we've not been properly introduced."

"Nor are we likely to be," she spat back.

"And yet, interestingly, you seem to know my name." He raised his eyebrows at her. "It hardly seems fair."

Muttering, "Cheeky bastard," she spun on her heels and, turning southwest, hurried away as fast as she could.

God, what a complete mess tonight had been. And she was running out of time. If Delacroix had heard that Sam possessed the letters, that meant the odious bastard was telling people about them in preparation for using them to blackmail the letter writers. She had to get them back before that happened or her father would become a laughingstock among his peers, and she would not let that happen. Augusta had caused him more than enough pain while she'd been alive. Nick wouldn't let the woman cause him any more harm now, even if it was just to his memory. She'd stop Sam anyway she could. And if Delacroix meant to use her mother's correspondence to do the same, well, she'd damn sure stop him too.

Chapter 4

Jack

Jack watched his ersatz rival stride off, feeling one of his unhealthy pangs of curiosity. The kind that inevitably got him involved in things over his head—but also occasionally provided him with an incredible opportunity. He unslung the rucksack he wore on his back and pulled out a warm scarf knitted by his aunts, each working from opposite ends towards the middle. The one who most accurately predicted the weather for the next day got to merge the pieces.

With a wry smile, he replaced his knit hat with a newsboy cap and tugged on a pair of fur-lined leather gloves. The mercury thermometer in the miniature Stevenson screen affixed outside the window of his rooms, an indulgence gifted to him by one of the handsome young gentlemen of a certain persuasion he referred to as patrons (because mark was such an ugly word), had read 1.9 degrees C when he'd left at midnight. Damn cold even for December and he missed the overcoat he'd eschewed in favor of nimbleness.

But the young woman he now considered following had to be even colder. That jumper looked thick and warm, but she wore no other outerwear, and that blueprint case she carried wouldn't keep her warm.

The leather container ranked high on Jack's curiosity meter too. What had she planned to take away in it? Sure, you could stuff a handful of letters in it, but you could do the same with a messenger bag or even a lady's drawstring purse. Why the tube?

He waited until she'd turned north into Great Cumberland Place, then strolled after her.

And thought about the first and only other time he'd seen her. Climbing through the third-story window of Lady Beatrice's bedroom at the exact moment he'd been preparing to leave in order to hand off the jewels he'd 'acquired' to an associate.

She'd worn trousers and what appeared to be the same black jumper and hat and had been so slight he'd assumed she was a lad. They faced each other, both shocked into immobility, and Jack found himself instantly entranced by a pair of the palest blue eyes he'd ever seen.

That little peccadillo had been in May. Now, he hurried after her as the streets grew narrower, and the neighborhood shifted from wealthy townhouses to solid middle-class places where a family might rent a small apartment of rooms. Jack had no permanent lodgings in the city, preferring to stay at his club, the Oxford and Cambridge University Club. The snobbery was astounding, but it allowed him easy access to the people from whom he made his various livings.

She'd been spitting mad that night at Lady Bea's. Hadn't taken well to his snaffling the jewels out from under her. And she couldn't have been sneaking in through the lady's bedroom window, dressed like a thief, for any other reason. He remembered stepping out of her way as she climbed in, then disappearing through the aperture with a whispered parting shot. "Better luck next time."

Tonight had apparently been next time. And neither of them had gotten away with the goods.

Who was she? She clearly knew him; she'd called him by name. And he would have remembered meeting a woman with those unforgettable eyes.

Half an hour later, she turned a final corner and marched up three steps to a modest but well-maintained house that contained several family apartments. The door opened before she'd even put her key in the lock, and she hurried inside, leaving Jack with only a brief glimpse of a tall, elderly man in a long nightshirt and cap.

He committed the street name and house number to memory, then started the long trek home. Tomorrow, he'd make it his business to find out who lived at No. 72 Bellingham Close. He needed to learn what interest this lady thief had in Augusta Byrne's scandalous letters. After all, a professional made it a rule to know his competition, and Jack always behaved professionally, no matter which of his many lines of "work" he engaged in.

Personal curiosity had nothing to do with this.

And if he believed that, he was as delusional as his two potty aunts.

Chapter 5

Nicola

"That bloody arse!" Nick dropped into one of two uphol-stered chairs in front of the fireplace in the parlor and flung off her boots.

Creighton, once her father's valet, and before that, his batman during the Crimea, retrieved her footwear, or as he called them, her manky boots, and set them on the little rug by the door. "Were you successful?"

"No."

Despite being dressed in his nightshirt and pom-pom bedecked nightcap, he exuded butler-like poise when he served her a glass of whiskey. Only his eyes betrayed his concern. "I am sorry, Miss Nick. And by 'bloody arse', I assume you mean Mr. Byrne?"

"No, I bloody don't." She didn't need to look up from rubbing her aching feet to see him frown at her language. She knocked back the whiskey and handed him the glass. He didn't refill it. "It was *him*. That idiot I encountered last spring at Lady Beatrice's. Jack Delacroix."

"Ah." A pause, then, "Did Mr. Delacroix acquire the letters, then?"

"No." Nick gestured to the other chair. "Oh, do sit down, Creighton."

He ignored her, as he always did. He'd die with that great butler-y stick up his arse. "So Mr. Byrne still retains the goods."

"Yes." She leaned back in the chair, which, with its twin, she'd taken from the attic at her father's house when she'd learned her uncle had inherited the property and planned to evict her. She'd always had to plan ahead. It had become a hallmark of her life.

Pressing her fingers against eyes that watered only because she was so tired, she sighed. "For now. But I'll get them. I swear to you, I'll get them."

She stretched her hands toward the coals still glowing in the grate. "I'll go again. Tomorrow night."

"Ah." How did he manage to convey so many emotions with just one syllable? Did they teach that in valet school? Was there a valet school? This "ah" held a tone of disapprobation. "Tomorrow night is Lady Emily's holiday masquerade ball."

"Oh, bollocks."

"Miss Nicola! Really, such language."

She smiled fondly at him. Despite no longer living in a stately home and now unable to work for a respectable family, he would still maintain his hard-won standards and hold her to them as well. "My apologies."

"Lady Emily sent a package for you. I have placed it on your bed. The enclosed note indicates it is your costume."

She groaned. "I never told her I'd go."

"She expressed her joy at the expectation of seeing you there and mentioned the great pains she took in selecting the perfect costume for you."

"She would." Nick groaned. Em's choice of costume was guaranteed to set Nick's hair on fire. Probably Cleopatra or the Queen of Sheba or some other obnoxiously feminine character. Nick rubbed her face and wiped away the night's frustrations. Reinforcing her weariness, the little ormolu clock that had once sat on the mantle in her father's study chimed three.

Sleep. She needed sleep. She'd worry about that ridiculous ball tomorrow. Who had costume balls at Christmas, anyway? "I'm for bed. Thank you, Creighton." She stood and bussed him on the cheek, taking him by surprise. "For everything."

A fond smile cracked that supercilious butlery face. "Good night, Miss."

She disappeared into her bedroom, and stripped, leaving her clothes where they fell. She crawled into bed with a sigh, burrowing under the covers, still cozy from the bedwarmer. God bless that old fool. When her uncle had sacked the staff after his brother had died, Nick had done her best to find new positions for most of them, but Creighton was so old, he positively creaked. So she'd kept him with her.

Sam, of course, had believed she'd never be able to keep a roof over her own head, much less afford to care for someone else. He salivated, waiting for her to come crawling back so he could bully her into marrying one of his cronies.

But Sam didn't know her. Nor that she'd spent the last ten years learning a host of skills, none of them designed to win her an eligible bachelor. She could neither embroider nor use a hand fan to suggest an assignation in the garden, but she could climb to a third-floor balcony and pick just about any lock. She also knew paste from real gems, could identify a grandmaster from a cheap knock-off, and outrun any copper she'd ever been chased by.

No, she was no longer rich, and she didn't much care to be. But she could keep herself and Creighton housed, fed, and reasonably warm in the winter, which none of her former female friends could say for themselves.

She drew in a long, slow breath and let it out. She'd get those letters back. Maybe not tomorrow, but before Sam could make use of them. And she'd do it before that jumped-up French-Irish dandy Jack Delacroix could take another crack at them, too.

Eventually she drifted into a hazy dream, wherein a tall, lean man with sherry brown eyes and the devil's own smile swept off a knit cap, revealing a sweep of silken black curls that framed an angel's face.

Her eyes flew open. Damn that man! She wiped the vision from her mind, slapped a pillow over her head, and forced herself back to sleep.

Chapter 6

Jack

Jack had only just crossed the threshold of his club when the night porter hurried across the marble-tiled hall toward him. In a hushed voice, he said, "I'm sorry, sir, but an urgent telegram came for you a few hours ago."

Jack sighed and took the proffered missive. "Thank you, Hargreaves."

"Of course, sir." A pause. Despite his name, Hargreaves was barely out of the spotty, gawky years, with a shock of red hair and a swath of freckles across his cheeks, far younger than the usual curmudgeonly staff that haunted the club's front hall. "I hope it's not about your aunts, sir."

It like as not was. Every time one of these telegrams came, Jack's heart stopped, fearing the worst. Mostly, the reason for the urgent notes came down to neediness and the ridiculous things his elderly relatives considered emergencies. But one day it might prove more ominous news.

Jack tore open the envelope and scanned the few words printed on the folded page.

"Come at once. Most urgent. Love, M & M"

He glanced up at Hargreaves. "I suppose you'd best call me a cab to Charing Cross Station."

"Right away, sir."

Jack glanced at his watch. Nearly four in the morning. The first train out usually departed about half six. Two and a half hours to York, another hour by carriage to the old pile, call it eight hours to deal with the crise du jour, then the same amount of time back…God, it was going to be a long one. And if he recalled correctly, Lady Emily's Christmas Masquerade ball was tonight. He considered sending his regrets, but there would be many wealthy members of the aristocracy there, some of whom he knew, and some of whom might be worth knowing. And it had taken him four months to get close enough to the soiree's hostess to curry an invitation.

No, by God, he needed to go to this ball. He'd just have to sleep on the train.

Intermittent watery sunshine broke through the thin cloud cover and dappled the snow-covered moors. Somehow, the sky seemed bigger here than it did in London. Some of Jack's school chums found it overwhelming, a sort of reverse claustrophobia, but it felt like home to Jack. It was London he often found too close, too busy, too noisy.

He wrapped up tightly in the lap rug as the wind whistled around the open carriage. The snow-packed road muffled the rhythmic clopping of the horse's hooves, lulling him into a drowse again.

He woke with a start as the vehicle jerked to a stop and old Archie, the carriage driver, called out, "Here we are, Mr. Jack. Brandimore House, same as you left it."

"Thanks, Arch. Hey to the missus." Jack jumped to the ground, threw the borrowed lap rug onto the seat, and with a wave, trudged up the drive to what his aunts called "la maison" through the snow.

The front door opened a crack as he drew close, and the groundskeeper, Hugo, peered out with a suspicious glare. Jack called a greeting and stomped off the worst of the clumps of white on the stoop before entering.

"Took your time, boy."

Jack tried to keep from his voice the panic that he'd held at bay all morning. "They're well? No one's ill?"

"Right as rain. But they've been fretting, what with you takin' so long."

Relieved, Jack took no offense at the older man's gruff demeanor. That was just Hugo. Jack might have explained that there was no midnight train from London to York, or that he actually had a life there and didn't sit waiting on his hands for emergency telegrams, but it would have been a waste of breath. Besides, Hugo, along with his wife, Mrs. E, took care of the house and its occupants. If it weren't for them, Jack could never have gone off to Cambridge, and later to London, and they'd all be living in some squalid cold-water flat in Cheapside.

So Jack thanked Hugo and brushed past him and into the morning room, where his aunts no doubt awaited him with coffee and croissants.

"Jacques! Mon Dieu! We were so worried. What kept you so long?"

"Bonne matin, Tante Madeleine." He hurried across to the elder of the two sisters and took her hands, kissing her cheeks. Though she had a full head of luxuriant blond and silver hair, today she wore a wig that wouldn't have looked out of place on Marie Antoinette. How she kept the tall, ornate thing on without a strap tied under her chin, Jack had no idea. She'd powdered her face as well and rouged her lips and cheeks. For a woman of seventy-something, she remained in remarkable health, and her eyes sparkled with lively intelligence.

He turned to next to Matilde, who stood in front of the French doors that led to their small, formal garden, now blanketed with two feet of snow. Matilde, younger than Madeleine by some years, had eschewed the affectation of her antique wig, choosing to wear her light, gray-streaked brown hair in a soft chignon. Her pink cheeks owed nothing to cosmetics. Though less outgoing than her sister, the same spark shone in her eyes.

Jack kissed her cheeks, too. "Tante Matilde. You're looking well." Thank God, he thought. He knew that one day he'd come home to find one of them had genuinely fallen ill. He could only hope that day was decades away.

"Bonjour, ma chou. We've missed you so. You haven't been up in weeks and weeks. And you look hungry."

It had only been nine days. But he was ravenous.

Matilde called out through the open parlor door. "Bess! Petit dejeuner, s'il vous plait. Jacques a faim!" She pointed to the little table where the ladies usually had their breakfast. Abandoning her native tongue, she ordered him to sit. "You've dark circles under your eyes, mon chou. Did we call you away from something?"

He didn't sit. He needed to find out what they wanted, other than his company. There was always something, no matter how manufactured it might be. "Nothing as important as seeing you. But your telegram said there was something urgent?"

Madeleine pointed across the long room where Jack saw a tall, robust pine tree propped against the wall. "Just look, Jacques. Look at that paltry thing."

He didn't sigh, just stared at the tree. It had to be at least nine feet tall, and had it not been crammed in a corner, the bottom boughs would be a full five feet in diameter. "Paltry?"

"It is pitiful. Unacceptable. Impossible. You must go at once to Mr. Merrithew and have him take it back and bring us a proper tree. It is only two days until Christmas, and we have so much decorating to do."

What she meant was that Hugo and Mrs. E had so much to do under the aunts' careful supervision.

"It looks like a splendid tree to me."

"Non. Non, non, non. C'est la catastrophe!"

He walked over to the tree and, hands clasped behind his back, pretended to examine the offending conifer. "I see. Yes. Yes, you are quite right."

Madeleine beamed at him. "Do you see, Tilly? Our Jack will take care of everything, just like he always does."

Jack nodded. "Anything for the two most beautiful women in the world." He went to the door and called for Hugo, who stood in the hall adjusting a painting that was not askew. "Hugo, could you please send for Mr. Merrithew? I'll meet with him in the study, and we'll get this sorted out."

Hugo groused, as he always did, and in due course, after Mrs. E had stuffed Jack with food, Merrithew showed up.

Three hours later, with the unacceptable tree hauled from the parlor, dragged behind the house, then dragged back in as though it were a new tree and pronounced by both aunts as wonderful, Jack made his way back to the train station in York and from there to London.

In his rooms, he found a package from Lady Emily; the costume she had arranged for him. Pulling it out, he smiled. He'd be Harlequin that night, a character from the commedia dell'arte. A rogue, a bit of a womanizer, and a general pain in the arse to the more serious Pierrot. And lover of the delectable vamp, Columbine. So that's the game his lovely hostess wanted to play. Well, he'd made love to many married women over the years. And she was delightful. But he'd not gotten the sense she'd been interested in such an affaire de coeur during their various encounters over the last few months.

With a shrug, he set the costume on the bed and readied himself for the ball. He needed to meet briefly with a contact before tonight's soiree, so he'd be a bit more than fashionably tardy. But that could work to his advantage. A late entrance often made for one without competition for attention. Let the games begin.

Chapter 7

Nicola

Nick arrived early at the Belgravia townhouse of her dearest friend Em, now *Lady* Emily since her marriage to the handsome and dashing Captain Sir Gideon Shelbourne two years ago in May. With the costume still wrapped in a bundle under Nick's arm, and a small carpet bag containing her mother's pearl-bedecked hair combs and the remnants of her cosmetics, Nick allowed herself to be ushered up the stairs into Emily's large suite and suffered an immediate onslaught of hugs by Nell.

When her uncle had sacked the majority of the servants upon moving in, Nick had found a place with Emily for the young woman who'd been Nick's own lady's maid. A perfect arrangement since, before Emily's marriage, she and her mother had shared a maid and Emily was currently without. Tonight, Nell would prepare them both for the festivities.

Nick would rather have stood in Caesar's place in the Curia of Pompey and gotten knifed than have her hair fussed with and cosmetics slapped onto her face, but there was no help for it. Modern society ran on rules and expectations, especially for women. One more reason she preferred to present as a man when she could get away with it. Well, not a man, perhaps. Just not a frilly girl. But still.

When Nell had hugged her long enough and hard enough to break ribs, it was Emily's turn. Em gave her a gentle squeeze, then took her by the shoulders and eyed her appraisingly.

"You've lost weight."

Nick shrugged out of Em's grasp. "The benefits of an active lifestyle." She too looked her friend up and down. Em's cheeks were pink, and maybe a little fuller. In fact, she looked a little fuller everywhere. Not unhealthily so, but... "Oh my God, Em. Are you...?"

Emily clapped her hands, her eyes shining. "Yes!" Her hand went to her belly. "We haven't announced it yet. Too soon. Anything could happen at this stage. But hopefully, in just about six months, Shel and I will be parents. Can you believe it?"

"That's...amazing!" Nick tried to project the same level of excitement and joy she knew her friend felt. Inside, though, her mood deflated like a leaky dirigible. Em was her last friend. They'd seen so much less of each other since the marriage, and now her life would revolve around her little bundle of joy.

As if sensing Nick's thoughts, Em took her hand. "I know. But you wouldn't be so lonely if you'd find someone for yourself."

Nick barked a laugh. "Right. Because I'm so eminently marketable."

"I can name at least half a dozen men who'd propose in a heartbeat if you'd give them the slightest nudge." She dragged Nick down to sit on the edge of the bed. "In fact, in addition to the usual lot, all of whom you've rejected by now, I've got three new bachelors to tantalize you with tonight."

"Oh, God. I knew I should have begged off."

"Wait, just listen. First, there's Martin Wheatley. He's the second son, just come back from four years in South Africa. Dashingly handsome with thick wavy blond locks, piercing blue eyes, and owns his own diamond mine. Not being the primary heir, there's no title, but he's dripping in money and good looks. Plus, Shel says he's a really good egg."

Oh, well, if Shel said so. Nick refrained from pulling a face. "I don't need to be Lady Anything. Nor do I need someone to serve me diamonds morning, noon, and night."

"I knew you'd say that. Okay, how about a charming American? Lyle Brookfield, scion of the New York Brookfields. You know, the shipping magnate? Owns a gigantic mansion in someplace called Long Island and a swank apartment in New York City. Very tall, with a daring mustache, and dresses better than Beau Brummel."

Nick groaned. "Probably spends all his money on clothes and has a lecherous father whom I'd spend all my days sliding away from. Em, please. Just stop. I don't need a husband."

"You really are impossible to please. But I think you'll find bachelor number three too hard to resist. I mean, if I weren't already married to the most handsome and wonderful man in the world, I'd go after this one myself. Now, he's a little cash poor, but he does have a title, although it's a French one, so that hardly counts. Comte something or other. Still. He's utterly gorgeous and dripping with charm. Has a rambling old place in Yorkshire where his two aunts live. Sad story, really. Margaret Swinton had it from some folks up north that his parents died young and tragically, and the old biddies took him in. From all reports, he's devoted to them, which is sweet. And bonus, no lewd paternal figure to avoid."

"Em—"

"Look, this one's different. Educated at Cambridge, but not one of the same boring old chaps in our set. He's a bit of a rogue, actually, but I think he's just biding his time, waiting for the right woman."

"Which you think is me."

"I do. Look, you're both rebels. You both have a wicked sense of humor, and you both hate society's rules. You're perfect for each other."

Nick considered how rude it would be to run for the door now. Yet Em was her best friend. The only friend who'd stood by her after her uncle had turned her out, left her destitute save for the small annuity from her father, and ostracized her from her own social class. She had so little left to lose. She wasn't sure she could bear losing Em, too. "Fine. I'll do what's expected. But I don't have to like it. Or them."

"Good. At least try to have a little fun, eh? It's nearly Christmas. And it's a ball!" She kissed Nick's cheek. "Now, let's get you all dolled up. You'll be Columbine. I picked out a gorgeous costume for you. And you'll know Monsieur le Comte because he'll be—"

"Oh, let me guess," Nick said in a positively Saharan tone. "He'll be Harlequin."

"Mais bien sûr!" Em giggled and gave her a side hug. "Oh, come on, Nick. Drink a little champagne, dance a few minuets, canoodle with a couple of handsome men in the garden, and at midnight scamper back to your strange new life and do whatever it is you do."

The thieving was the one thing Nick hadn't shared with Em. Too dangerous for both of them. Nor had she told her friend about her mother's letters. The fewer who knew about those, the better. "I guess when you put it that way, what have I got to lose?"

Em beamed and led Nick to the vanity stool before gesturing at Nell. "Wonderful! Let's get started!"

The ballroom on the third floor felt a lot like a sardine tin by ten pm. Nick had been duly introduced to both the incredibly boring Captain Wheatley, whose idea of whispering sweet nothings consisted of long, tedious tales of killing natives and ordering workers about in a mine, and the equally appalling American chap, who talked nonstop for nearly an hour about stocks and the buying and selling of them, and of all the swank art pieces his mother had purchased on their last trip to Italy, as though that somehow made up for his lack of breeding.

She'd danced with—and had her feet trampled by—a number of other young men, most of whom she knew. Her face hurt from faking a smile for hours, her eyes burned from far too little sleep, and her repertoire of small talk had dried up like those poor South African natives under the burning sun.

At midnight, while the musicians were on a break, she slipped away from Gavin Holcombe, who, at thirty-five, still had not found a woman to marry him. He was nice enough. Nice like toast. Toast without marmalade. Just plain, boring, pale, dry toast. And he didn't have enough money for most of his potential fiancées to make up for it. Excusing herself from Gavin's offer of another glass of champagne, she left the ballroom to "powder her nose" and made a beeline for a small, private salon which opened onto a balcony overlooking the gardens. Although her costume bared her shoulders, and the temperature had dropped into single digits, she needed air.

The salon was rather dimly lit, and she noticed a number of couples entwined together in various corners or on scattered settees, but she paid them no mind, nor they her, and she slipped out the French doors without being hailed. Maybe it was all the champagne she'd drunk, maybe it was the dozens of bodies crowding the ballroom, but the chill bite of December felt good against her skin. She strolled to the railing and leaned on it, taking deep breaths.

Muffled sounds of revelry leaked out to her. Most of the guests had also imbibed too much champagne by now, and as this was a youngish crowd, no stodgy oldsters attended to dash cold water on the festivities. Somehow, out here under the blanket of fluffy gray clouds, she could enjoy the babble of conversations and the bursts of laughter far better. It's how she'd enjoyed most things in her life since her father's death—just slightly to one side.

A spattering of wet, heavy snowflakes began to fall, and in the darkness and solitude, she lifted her face to catch the fat flakes on her tongue. A giggle escaped as a childhood memory struck her of playing in the snow with her father, making snow angels and flinging snowballs at one another. They'd had hot cocoa after, snuggled in blankets by the fire in his study, and since her mother had been visiting friends in Paris, no one even groused about the snowy tracks they'd made tromping through the house.

The first she knew she was no longer alone on the balcony was when someone leant on the rail next to her.

"I suppose ten other men tonight have told you how lovely you are when you smile."

She turned, saw the man in the Harlequin costume and groaned. "You."

"And you." His voice was a little breathy, and his eyes held amusement. "I had assumed our hostess would be my Columbine, but I am delighted to find it is you instead."

She tried to work up annoyance but found herself too tired. "Your hostess is a married woman." A pregnant married woman.

"She is indeed. And you? Has a handsome but dreadfully prosaic Pierrot claimed your heart?" His normally flippant tone—if she could claim to know what was normal for him after two brief exchanges—had morphed into something more thoughtful.

She smiled despite herself. Clearly too much champagne. "This Columbine is a free spirit. I have no Pierrot to tie me down."

That soft smile reached those remarkable eyes, the color of fine cognac. Must be his French heritage. "I'm delighted to hear that. May I have the next dance?"

Muted music filtered out from the ballroom. She looked at the French doors to the salon, loath to go back inside, despite the cold now making her shiver.

He followed her gaze. "We can dance here, if you prefer. But first..." he swept off the short cape he wore over Harlequin's usual parti-colored jacket and draped it over her shoulders. "You've got to be freezing."

The cloak still retained the heat from his body, and she let out an involuntary sigh. Damn, she should not have had those last two glasses of champagne. She should be hurrying inside after giving him a snide comment. But when he extended a hand in invitation, she took it.

He swung her through a sedate waltz, constrained by the small confines of the balcony. Held her not too tightly, yet close enough she felt the warmth radiating from him, smelled his aftershave, enjoyed the feel of firm muscular shoulders slide beneath the silk of his costume doublet.

He was, in all honesty, the best dance partner she'd ever had.

When the musicians stopped, she almost regretted it. And when he led her to the snow-covered stone bench and brushed off the few flakes that had landed there in the protected alcove, she didn't decline sitting with him, even recognizing how compromised she was, and knowing she'd regret it in the morning.

But that was then, and this was now, and for the first time since her father died, she felt relaxed and on the verge of enjoying herself.

"So, you," he murmured. His gaze rested upon her face, not, as had happened all evening, on her decolletage. And when he spoke, he surprised her again. Instead of a litany about himself, he said, "Tell me about you."

Chapter 8

Jack

Jack leaned in, and despite his normally cynical nature, felt a thrill of anticipation for her to speak. For her to share something, anything, genuine. And for once, he had no desire to use that disclosure for his own ends. He just wanted to know more about her.

Her lips parted, those crystal blue eyes met his, and he found himself breathless. The moment hung there between them. It would be so easy to close the distance, pull her close by the capelet he'd given her, and kiss those lips. He could almost taste them, feel their softness against his own mouth.

If only that brief interlude had lasted an instant longer.

Her voice broke the spell. "I'm nothing special, Mr. Delacroix. Despite being a friend of Lady Emily, I have nothing in which you'd be interested." She gestured to the sapphire necklace that glittered against the bare skin of her throat. "These are hers, not mine."

His lips quirked up. "They are also paste. But I know you're aware of that, too." He adjusted the cape on her shoulders, clasping it closed in front, covering the necklace, and the slim, pale curve of her shoulders. "That's not what I'm after. I honestly want to know you better. What you like to do. What things make you smile. Other than catching snowflakes on your tongue."

She glanced aside, and he wondered if it was the champagne she'd clearly indulged in or something else that brought a flush to her cheeks. When she met his eyes again, some of the alcohol fog had cleared. "You don't even know my name."

"So tell me that, at least." They both knew he could find out.

She lifted her chin. "Nicola." She paused as though making a decision, then plunged forward. "Nicola Byrne."

A jolt of recognition sizzled up his spine. Byrne? *The* Nicola Byrne?

He saw in her face the instant his recognition of her name showed on his face. Apparently, his fatigue had impaired his ability to hide his feelings. A wall slammed down between them, and her gaze frosted over, her eyes becoming the pale blue of sea ice.

He swallowed. Tried to recover the moment. "Allow me to offer my condolences on the death of your father."

"A little late for that. But thank you."

She'd grown positively glacial.

He had more questions for her now, not one of which was personally motivated. The first one slipped past his guard and out of his mouth before he could stop it. "What were you doing in your former home last night?"

"None of your business." In her lap, her hands clenched into fists. "I'll ask you the same question."

"May I be frank with you?"

The ice cracked a bit, and a smile slipped past her own guard. "You can be anyone you choose, Mr. Delacroix. And I prefer frankness to games, which I understand you play exceedingly well."

"I see my reputation precedes me. Something for which I'm not sure I'm sorry. Games become tedious. It's rare that I can be myself." He wished he'd had more champagne himself. Then he could blame the urge to kiss her on the booze. Instead, he eased back and with incredible reluctance removed his hands from the capelet. If he'd been on the hunt, he'd have pressed forward. She was vulnerable, and more than a little drunk.

Yet he wanted to give her space.

"I was there for the same reason you were. The letters. Your uncle plans to use them to extort certain individuals for favors, exceptions, the usual sorts of things."

"And you'd like to do the same." Her cheeks flamed red, and her eyes flashed in anger.

"Not precisely. I have no need for political favors or get-out-of-jail-free cards for my nefarious underlings. I have no underlings and were I ever to be captured by the coppers, I'd submit quietly and do my time. Anything to avoid a scandal. I have two elderly aunts, and I couldn't bear for them to be affected by my...extracurricular activities. What I do need is an income."

"So why are you a thief? Why not work an honest job?"

He chuckled. "Me? A useless playboy living on a meager inheritance from my mother? Who on earth would hire me? And you must know how expensive it is to maintain an ancient, creaking family estate. The old pile is a falling down mess. The roof needs repairing, one wing of the house is completely uninhabitable, the brick needs tuck pointing, the pipes need replacing..." He sighed. "It's all I can do to keep my aunts in tea, biscuits, and a Sunday roast."

"You could move them to a smaller place. It happens to the best of us."

He knew she spoke from experience. And oh, how often he'd considered that very thing. But the illegitimate offspring of Marie Antoinette's brother (or uncle, or cousin, the relationship depended on the day and how many glasses of sherry Madeleine had imbibed) could reside in nothing smaller or grander than the house they'd inhabited in since they'd first come to this country as children. He couldn't do that to them. It would shatter their illusions, the only thing that kept them going. They'd been through so much during their harrowing escape from France in the days after Napoleon's final defeat. They'd lost nearly everyone and everything on that winter channel crossing.

He pinched the bridge of his nose. The pressure of the line he walked, the push and pull of presenting himself as a young, wealthy scion of the now extinct French aristocracy, while sneaking off with his patroness du jour's family jewels, weighed on him tonight like never before.

It had to be exhaustion, and a niggle of fear wormed its way in. Was he getting too old for this? For the chase? For the thievery? He'd be thirty next year. Damn it, he had to get his hands on those letters. They could be his retirement strategy.

Nicola watched him expectantly, and he didn't have to feign a tired exhale. "I could move the old dears. But it would break their hearts. And maybe their spirits. They've been very good to me and doing that would be a heartless way to repay them."

A little more of that wall of ice melted away, despite her crisp words. "As an excuse for criminal behavior, two beloved and aged aunts is certainly novel. Usually, I hear about dear old mum wasting away from a terrible illness, or sparing granddad, an old war veteran suffering from terrible battle wounds."

She appeared to be almost as brittle and cynical as he was. The irony made him want to crack that bitterness like a hollow chocolate egg to expose the sweetness he imagined lived inside, to make her smile the way she had in that unguarded moment he witnessed when he'd come out onto the balcony.

He shook his head. Good God, what was wrong with him? He refocused. "So what would you have done with those letters? Burn them to spare your mother's reputation?"

Her laugh dripped with acrimony. "Not blooming likely. Augusta Newton Byrne made her bed, she can bloody well continue lie in it. I'd burn them, yes. And I will. But not for her."

"For you then?" Did she hope to salvage her own reputation, now tainted by her scandal of a mother and an uncle who was the undisputed crime lord of London?

"No. Not for me. I've made peace with whom and what I am now. I've never cared for the role foisted upon me by my gender and class."

"Then why...oh." He leaned forward again to peer into those remarkable eyes, whose gaze could give a man's soul frostbite from the cold anger burning in them. "Your father."

She jerked back as though he'd slapped her. She mastered her shock and surprise at his guess in seconds, but the wall she'd built shattered into icy shards. She looked suddenly younger and far more vulnerable.

She got to her feet a little unsteadily and tossed his capelet onto the bench. "Thank you for the loan. Goodnight, Mr. Delacroix."

He stood as well. He wanted to grab her, keep her with him, make her talk to him. But he knew better. "It's Jack. My name is Jack. May I call you Nicola?"

She'd expected something more forceful from him, he realized. Had wanted, he thought, for him to physically prevent her from leaving so she could rail against him. "My friends call me Nick. *You* can call me Miss Byrne. Or perhaps just not call me at all."

She swept inside, head held high, a bundle of conflicting emotions surrounded by puzzles he was dying to solve.

To what end? said the more pecuniary part of his brain. She was penniless, not the kind of woman—or young man, in a pinch—he usually went after. She had no wealth, no family jewels, no antiques, no priceless art, no acquaintances who could further Jack's own ends.

And yet.

He stood and watched as she hurried past the trysting couples in the salon and into the hallway beyond, heading right to who knew where instead of left to the ballroom. He rescued the discarded capelet, yet remained on the balcony, shivering in the cold, frozen not by the temperature or the fat lazy snowflakes that dusted his hair and his costume, but by fascination. Several minutes passed before he slipped back inside, icy fingers pressed against his lips where the non-existent kiss they might have shared somehow burned like fire.

Chapter 9

Nicola

Nick hurried up the back stairs to Emily's suite of rooms. She couldn't wipe the memory of Jack's intent gaze, or the curve of his smile, or the feel of his hand against the small of her back as they danced. Thank heavens she'd realized how close she'd been to kissing him. Worst of all, she knew now for certain he was after her mother's letters.

She hated the notion that she'd let him affect her so. Clearly, he meant to use her in some way. That was how men like that operated. Thinking only of their own ends; she had experience aplenty with that sort and often used their predilections to *her* own ends. And yet she'd wanted to kiss him. All while wanting to dislike him. The feelings were discordant and contradictory, and the only way to resolve them in the moment had been to find a reason to get angry and leave.

Reaching Em's rooms, she divested herself of the costume and resumed her own clothes. Dashing a quick note thanking Em for a "lovely evening", and congratulating her again on her condition, she took the back stairs and slipped out through the kitchen door. When she reached the street without meeting a single soul, she breathed a sigh of relief. The music and chatter from inside had become little more than a muted buzz. Carriages lined the streets, their horses dozing while waiting to take party-goers home, and their drivers and footmen clustered together behind a screen of bushes along the side of the house, smoking cigarettes and exchanging gossip.

Nick made her silent way down the street, hugging the shadows for a block, doing her best to remain invisible. In addition to not wanting the gossipers to see her, a woman out alone at this hour made herself a target for all sorts of difficulties. And while she could fend off the worst of them if she had to, that too would draw unwanted attention. A rush of relief relaxed her shoulders when she rounded the first corner—until she saw a hansom cab waiting at the curb.

Jack Delacroix leaned out of the open door of the brougham. "May I escort you home?"

She should refuse. Despite the danger of walking alone. Despite the cold. How had he known where she'd be or that she'd be leaving? Damn the man.

He hopped out of the carriage. He'd changed from his costume as well and wore a pair of tweed trousers under a heavy topcoat. "It's a long walk, it's bitterly cold, and extremely dangerous this time of night." When she continued to stare at him like an addlepated ninny, he added, "Please. Let me do this. By way of apology for upsetting you."

Every instinct screamed at her to run the other way. Delacroix himself could be dangerous. She could be accepting a ride from exactly the sort of villain he warned her about. Yet something deeper, something more intuitive, told her Jack wasn't that kind of man. "I have a knife," she heard herself say.

"I believe you. I swear on my honor to be a gentleman."

"And your word is worth what, exactly?" But she stepped forward and allowed him to hand her into the carriage and settle a plaid lap robe over her legs.

What would have been an hour walk home took less than fifteen minutes by carriage. She didn't ask how he knew her address. He'd probably asked Em, and Em, being a consummate matchmaker, had spilled not only that, but probably a bunch of other personal tidbits. Arriving, he'd handed her out, then waited for her to unlock the door.

She turned back to him, her hand on the doorknob. "Thank you." She'd meant to stop there, but her mouth had other ideas. "Both for the ride and the dance."

He smiled, and her stomach jumped at both the charm of the expression and the genuineness she sensed. "I should be thanking you. It's not often I am able to simply be myself. I realize we are somewhat at odds professionally, but...I'd like to see you again. Perhaps a stroll through Regent's Park? All very proper."

Was this just an attempt to get her to relinquish her plan to reclaim the letters? If so, he was a fool. And much as she wanted him to be, she didn't believe he was. "Perhaps after this current business is over."

"I look forward to it, regardless of who wins." He paused, watching her. "You realize others may be after those documents, too. I only mention it to warn you. To be careful. I might be a thief, but I'm not a violent man. Others of our kind are not so...gentlemanly."

That hadn't occurred to her. Nor had she thought to question how Jack had found out about them. God, she was an idiot. "Thank you. Again. And good night."

She had just twisted the knob when the door flew open and Creighton, half-dressed in shirtsleeves and trousers, tumbled out onto the stoop and collapsed at her feet.

"Creighton!" She knelt beside him and lifted his head to her lap. Blood stained her gloves, covered the side of his face, quickly soaked her skirts.

"Miss...I tried...m'sorry." His eyes fluttered closed.

"Creighton? Who did this? Are they still inside?"

Jack knelt beside her, took Creighton's pulse. "Unconscious, but his pulse is strong." He called to the driver. "Get the gent and the lady inside the carriage. I'll be back in a moment." With a grim look, he hurried inside and pounded up the stairs to their rooms.

Nick helped the driver wrestle Creighton into the vehicle, then raced into the house after Jack.

The door to their apartment was open, the wood around the latch splintered. The small desk lamp glowed on the little round table by the window where she and Creighton ate their meals, and by the dim glow, she took in the devastation.

In the parlor, the armchairs lay overturned, the stuffing leaking through slashes in the upholstery. Her small bookcase lay face down, and her father's favorite tomes scattered across the Turkish carpet. The ormolu clock on the mantel lay on the grate, the works springing from the face. Her one painting, a Turner seascape, had been flung to the floor, the frame nothing but gilded kindling.

Worst of all, the small, spindly Christmas tree Creighton had found for them, decorated with a small box of ornaments Nick had rescued from the attic, had been torn apart, the glass ornaments crushed into powder under booted feet.

She stood for a moment, heart pounding, fighting tears. Fury churned in her gut.

A noise came from the larger of the two bedrooms, and she spun, the knife she always carried in her bag now in her hand.

Jack appeared in the door frame, hands raised. He quirked his eyebrows up. "You weren't joking."

"I never joke about weapons. The place is empty?"

"Yes. They've long gone. Your man must have been watching for your return and came down to warn you."

She moved toward the bedroom, but Jack blocked her way. "No. No point in you going in there. Nothing much left to save. Whoever it was, shredded your clothes with a knife or a pair of scissors, slashed the bedding and flung paint on the walls."

"And Creighton's room?"

"Don't go in there. It's where they must have attacked him. He was likely getting ready for bed. It's not pretty."

She tried to push past him, but he took her by the shoulders, gently but firmly. "Don't. I'm not protecting your womanly sensibilities, but really, you don't want that image in your head." He pulled a folded piece of paper from his coat pocket. "They left this for you, pinned to the pillow with a knife."

She snatched the note from his hand and took it over to the lamp to read it. "Stay away, girlie, or next time, it will be you." Girlie. The appellation her uncle used for her. An insult, a way to diminish her, and she despised it.

Jack scowled. "You can't stay here. And your man needs medical attention."

"I will not let that creature force me from my home." Again.

"Nick, he can get to you anytime he wants here. It's not safe, not for you or Creighton. Please. Let me help."

A thought crossed her mind that maybe Jack had arranged this to trick her into abandoning her attempts to get the letters. But no. He would have no way of knowing her uncle's pet name for her. She looked up at him and was startled by both the fear and tenderness in his eyes. "I have nowhere else to go."

He looked aside for a moment. "I know a place, somewhere even Sammy the Smoke would never think to look."

"Where?"

"Do you trust me?"

She no longer trusted anyone. Hadn't for a long time. "I don't suppose I have a choice."

He smiled again. "Have you ever seen the moors?"

"The moors?"

"My family home is there. A little distance from York. There's room for both you and Creighton."

"That's where your aunts live. I'd be an imposition."

"They will be delighted. They don't get much company. I warn you, it's not palatial in any sense of the word. Probably not what you're used to."

She gestured around her. "I don't exactly live in the lap of luxury." Was she crazy accepting his offer? For even considering it? Probably. But what other option did she have? She could possibly arrange to stay with Em, but if her uncle really wanted to hurt her, that would be the first place he'd look. Besides, that could put Em, Shel, and the not yet born child at risk. And she had to get Creighton somewhere safe. He was the closest thing to family she had left. She took a deep breath. "Thank you. I...don't understand why you're doing this."

"And you're suspicious as hell? I would be too. I don't even know why I'm doing it. But I promise I have no devious motives." He reached to turn off the gas lamp. "Let's go. We'll stop at a friend's place. He's a doctor and can examine Creighton. We'll bide our time there until we can head to Charing Cross Station. First train to York leaves at half six."

She stayed him from turning out the lamp. "Wait. I have some traveling money hidden in the kitchen."

"If they didn't find it. They've broken most of the crockery."

Her heart sank. It had taken a year to make this small flat a home. Now, almost everything they had lay shredded or broken.

With Jack carrying the gas lamp, they stepped into the narrow kitchen, shards of pottery and china crunching beneath their feet. Nick had to sweep broken glass from the small dry sink in order to climb atop it to reach a little decorative shelf upon which she'd placed a rather hideous ceramic chicken. It looked like a bit of tasteless tat, and the shelf was high enough to prevent casual examination.

Jack helped her down and pointed at the thing. "A chicken?"

"Our cook always used to talk about saving egg money." She shrugged. "What better place to store egg money than in a chicken?" She turned the ceramic creature upside down and stuck her fingers into the hole she'd carefully bored into the base. The little bag of coins and one last piece of her mother's jewelry still rested inside.

She waved it triumphantly. "Not as smart as they thought they were."

"Rather, you are simply cleverer."

"Given Sam's henchmen, that's not much of a compliment. But thank you." She handed him the bag. "'Here. For your aunts. And the leaky roof."

He opened the bag, examined the contents and then passed it back. "No. You keep it."

"I won't accept charity. I had plenty of offers when I got kicked out. I didn't take them then, and I won't now."

To his credit, he didn't sigh in exasperation. "All right. I'll take this for safekeeping and when you are done with my hospitality, we'll see what the reckoning is, and I'll return the remainder. Sound fair?"

"Eminently."

Still wondering if she was making a hideous mistake, she followed him from the house and out into the night.

Chapter 10

Jack

Jack, despite his upbringing, allowed Nick to pay for a first-class compartment on the train to York. Creighton's injuries, apart from the head wound, turned out to be mostly superficial. He'd ache for a few days from the beating he took, and Harley, who wasn't quite yet a doctor but would be soon enough, had said that head wounds bled profusely and that since Creighton had come to with all his wits intact, and experienced no visual disturbances, he'd likely mend in short order.

To Jack's eye, Nick seemed relieved, though she fussed over the elderly man like a daughter would her father. He'd clearly been an old family retainer that Nick had somehow managed to save from the poorhouse after Sammy the Smoke had taken over the Byrne estate. The fact that Byrne threw his own niece out into the cold appalled Jack. He'd heard through the grapevine that the niece had been given an ultimatum: Marry one of his cronies or pack a bag and go.

In this world, where women were little more than broodmares, it said a lot about Nick's character that she'd chosen to make a go of it on her own. Taking Creighton with her said even more.

He didn't know who had fallen asleep first, he or Nick, but both jerked awake when the conductor knocked on the door with a hearty, "York Station." Jack hadn't even noticed the train slow.

A stiff wind blew sleety snow sideways as they exited the compartment onto the platform. Jack ushered them around to the lee side and went in search of a carriage. Old Archie was there, as he was most mornings, and an hour later, nearly frozen stiff, they trooped through the kitchen door of Brandimore House.

Mrs. E, startled in the act of lighting the stove, let out a strangled cry. In her thick Scots accent, she said, "Och, ya nearly scared the life outta me, Master Jack." She eyed Creighton and Nick curiously. "And who's this you've brought through the servant's entrance?"

Creighton had held up well so far, but Jack noticed his face grew a little gray and his steps a bit wobbly as they'd marched up the long drive to the house. "Full introductions later, Mrs. E. Right now, I need you to prepare two rooms for Miss, um, Creighton and her grandfather, if you please. I'm just going to take them through to the morning room. Is there a fire laid?"

He saw Nick shoot him a curious glance but, thank God, the woman had the sense to keep her mouth shut. She had rather a lot of sense, something he liked about her immensely.

"Aye, o'course. Their nibs are still in there, bickering over the menu for Christmas Eve. Like we don't have the same thing every year."

His first two responses, "Again?" And "Still?" remained unspoken. "I see," was what came out of his mouth, followed by the customary response of, "I'll take care of it."

Mrs. E grinned. "Good lad. Bannocks and potato leek soup for luncheon. Be ready in two shakes."

Jack gave her cheek a kiss as he moved his weary travelers past. "You're a gem, Mrs. E."

In the morning room, which faced east and got the bulk of the sun, when there was any, he found his aunts still sitting at the breakfast table, but instead of squabbling over the holiday menu, they were pouring over the ancient family Bible, one of the few things that had survived the Channel crossing.

Since they'd slept their way north on the train, Jack had had no time to prepare his companions for his aunts' eccentricity. The Bible, therefore, sent an ominous shiver through him. They would be discussing genealogy. Which would lead to the conversation of their distant (or not so distant) relation, Marie Antoinette, a situation he did not want to toss Nick into without warning. Not if he wanted her to continue to tolerate his presence. And that, God help him, and for whatever reason, was something he increasingly did want.

He took Creighton by the arm and sat him in one of the wingback chairs by the crackling hearth, then faced his now curious relatives and cleared his throat. "Bonne matin, Tante Madeleine, Tante Matilde. May I present to you Mademoiselle Creighton and her grandfather, Monsieur Creighton, of London?"

Both of his aunts' eyes lit up. He could almost hear dozens of questions popping up in their heads like stoats in the tall grass on the moors. He had to get Nick out of there fast before the barrage started.

Madeleine inclined her head, topped by the tallest powdered and beribboned wig she possessed. Matilde also wore "court" dress, a pale blue satin and brocade gown with a low neckline and more yards of fabric in the train than in all the morning room's full-length drapes.

"Monsieur et Mademoiselle, welcome to Brandimore House. We are delighted to have you. Jacques—"

Jack knew better than to stop. "I'd ask you to please entertain Mr. Creighton for a few moments while I show the young lady a place where she can freshen up after our journey north. The fine gentleman was wounded last night fighting off some miscreants and is in need of a cup of tea and a rest by the fire."

There, that did it nicely. Both aunts nodded in a stately and elegant manner and murmured the usual exclamations of concern, their eyes alight with excitement and curiosity. Nick gaped at Jack as he took her arm and hustled her from the morning room. As they exited, he whispered tersely in her ear. "Just play along. Please. I'll explain in a minute, I promise."

"But Creighton..."

"He'll be just fine. They love fussing over people, especially wounded people. And there are a few things I need to tell you."

She eyed him with deep suspicion, and he saw how her hand crept to her bag, within which she kept her knife. But she followed him, and that, he thought, was victory enough for the moment.

Chapter 11

Nicola

Nick felt dazed. She shouldn't have slept on the train, but she hadn't been able to keep her eyes open as the clackety-clack of the wheels and the gentle rocking motion lulled her into slumber. Now she was muzzy-headed, and worry, anger and fear vied for dominance, clouding her judgment. She turned her emotions onto the only target present. "What do you want?"

Jack looked a little startled but quickly recovered his aplomb. At least he didn't smirk at her as some men did when faced with a woman's ire. "I suppose short and sweet is best. Won't you please sit?"

She crossed her arms. Whatever game he was playing, she wanted no part in it.

He took a breath, glanced back through the doorway, his tension crackling in the chill air. "As I'm sure you've noticed, now that you've seen them, my aunts are a bit...eccentric."

She'd taken in the powdered wig and the antique gown on the elder of the two. It had been hard *not* to notice that. "I assume they're not preparing for a costume ball as well?"

He met her eyes before his gaze skittered away again. "No. Matilde and Madelaine are...distantly related to Marie Antoinette."

She'd trained herself to keep emotions from her countenance, but some days she found it harder than others. She was pretty sure from his embarrassed expression that she'd failed now, too. "Marie Antoinette? *The* Marie Antoinette. The beheaded queen of France."

He cleared his throat. "Yes, as it were."

"And are they?"

He squared his shoulders. "It is a matter of some debate as to what that relationship is, but they are quite adamant about it." He gestured at the parlor. "Knowing this will explain the, uh, decor, and the topics of conversation that may arise during your stay."

He was, she realized, embarrassed. And as uncharitable as it was, she felt for the first time she had the upper hand with him. "So you hide your barmy aunts up here in York to preserve your reputation."

"No!" Genuine anger flashed in his eyes. "I don't hide them. They grew up in this house. They love it here. Which is why I work so hard to keep this place going."

She'd realized she'd crossed a line. And found the one thing this popinjay actually cared about. As insouciant as he was, he loved his aunts. Em was right. It was sweet. And...telling. "I'm sorry. That was unconscionably rude, especially after what you've done for Creighton and me." She examined the room's furnishings, which did have a distinctly French provincial flair. A far cry from her threadbare attic chairs and ceramic chicken, but still, nothing was new, and she could see the patina of not just age but neglect on the settee and the draperies.

And the house itself was enormous. "It must take a lot to keep this place up and running."

Some of his smugness returned to cover his discomfiture. "Indeed."

"And it was important to reveal this to me why?"

He stared at her now, flummoxed. "I...I just wanted you to understand. They're important to me. And if we—" He broke off, turned away, scrubbed his face. "Dear God, I'm tired. I don't even know what I'm saying." When he faced her again, he wore the charming bon vivant smile, and his tone had grown cool. "What I mean to say is that people can often be casually cruel to them, and I would appreciate it if you could refrain from challenging them about their claims."

A little resentment flared. Did he think she was that callous? Then again, he hadn't exactly seen her be otherwise. She nodded. "I won't. I promise. And thank you again for taking us in."

He spread his hands. "I did what any gentleman would have done." He licked his lips, clearly nervous and uncomfortable. "May I show you to your room? I imagine Mrs. E will have put you in the south room and Creighton in my grandfather's suite. You can freshen up before we eat."

She shook her head. If she sat down alone for five minutes, she'd fall asleep again. "No, let's rejoin the others. I want to keep an eye on Creighton."

He hesitated. "You look exhausted, Nick. It's not only Creighton I'm concerned for."

"I'll be fine. Perhaps we can all take a rest after our meal."

He didn't move, his cognac-colored eyes watching her intently. "You're not like any woman I've ever met."

She smiled now. He seemed to have that effect on her. "That's usually not a positive statement."

"I mean it as one, I assure you." He gave her a quaint little bow, one hand behind his back, and gestured toward the doorway. "After you."

When they returned to the morning room, the two aunts had pulled over chairs and sat in front of Creighton, still comfortably ensconced in the wingback with a cup of something in his lap. An animated discussion was in progress, and Creighton leaned forward conspiratorially as he said, "...torrid affair, from the tales my grandmother told us in her declining years. There is no documentation, of course, but my father bore such a great resemblance to the king that he was sent to France for a time until maturity somewhat modified his features." He looked up at Nick and winked at her.

Creighton.

Winked.

"Ah, Nicola. Come join us. Jacques, be a good lad and pull up another chair. We were just talking family histories."

Jacques?

Madeleine nodded vigorously and her enormous, powdered wig swayed dangerously. "We recognized the likeness immediately, of course."

Jack carried over two of the ladder-back chairs from the breakfast table. "Likeness?"

Matilde spoke. "Oh yes, don't you see it? He is the spitting image of George IV. We recognized his regal bearing the moment he walked in."

Nick felt Jack's hands on her shoulder, gently nudging her into the chair he'd placed behind her. "George," she echoed. "King George."

"No need to be coy, Nicola. I've told these ladies all about our family's little secret, as they saw the truth instantly. And of course, they have shared theirs, so it's all out in the open now. You're in the presence of royalty, luv. Mademoiselles Madeleine and Matilde are related to Marie Antoinette."

She stared at Creighton. Watched him wink at her again. Saw a broad smile on his normally serious face. And felt a bit like she had stepped into Lewis Carrol's *Alice in Wonderland*.

Matilde nodded, but her wig was not so tall as to risk toppling off her head. "Through our cousin on my father's side."

"No, no," Madeleine shot back. "It was the stepbrother, Tilly. Uncle Gustav."

"Papa said it was Cousin Ernst."

"Pah. Papa couldn't remember his own middle name after he was shot in the head outside of Calais."

"I don't remember him getting—"

"You were too young, Tilly. You can hardly be expected to remember much of that awful journey from Paris to Calais."

Tilly's mouth set. "You're right, of course, Maddy." But while Matilde demurred to her older sister, the look in her eyes told Nick she didn't agree on either point. And the pained look on Jack's face suggested this sort of thing, if not this specific squabble, was nothing new.

Nick hid a smile behind a cough and her hand.

Madeleine smiled up at Jack. "Given the way the monarchies intermarry, we might all be related." She gave Nick a curious smile. "Distantly, of course. Not enough to be a problem."

It was all Nick could do to nod politely. Fortunately, the discussion was interrupted by Mrs. E, who announced that luncheon would be served shortly in the dining room.

Jack, who still stood behind her chair, breathed a sigh. "Mr. Creighton, sir, do you feel well steady enough to join us, or should I have Mrs. E bring you a tray?"

Creighton set his cup on a little side table and stood briskly. "Fit as a fiddle, my boy, thanks to the kind attentions of you and your aunts." He crooked his arm at Nick. "May I escort you, Nicola?"

She stood with a look at Jack, who grinned at her. "Of course...Granddad."

By the time the simple but delicious meal had been consumed, and Jack had escorted her and Creighton to their rooms, Nick found herself close to hysteria, not sure whether to laugh or cry. That had to have been the strangest meal of her life, and yet, the zaniness had felt wonderfully free of all her everyday problems. Maybe it was better to live a life where the impossible and the unlikely painted your world with bright colors.

She flopped onto her back on the rather lumpy but enormous platform bed and stared up at the blue silk canopy high overhead, dotted artfully with silver fleur-de-lis. A bed fit for a princess, she thought. If Jack's aunts' beliefs held true, did that mean Jack was actually some kind of French royalty? Not that there was royalty there anymore. Still, would his wife become some sort of princess?

Good heavens, she'd been infected by whatever insanity ran rampant here. She was the daughter of a professor and the niece of a crime lord, not the illegitimate descendant of George IV. Nor was she ever likely to be anyone's wife.

But, argued a little voice, if an enchanted frog girl kissed a prince, might she not become a princess?

Hah. Maybe. In this house.

She started to laugh and couldn't stop for a long time. When the fit finally ended, she rolled over on her side and, still smiling, closed her gritty, tired eyes and drifted into a doze—broken all too soon by a muffled rapping on her door.

"Nick," came the terse whisper. "Nick, let me in. It's urgent."

Chapter 12

Jack

Jack slipped inside as soon as Nick opened the door. She looked rumpled, wisps of hair pulled loose from her damaged coiffure from the previous night. Her eyes held a bleary, half-dazed expression. She'd clearly fallen asleep. Ridiculously, he found he wanted to tuck those wisps behind her ears, lead her back to the bed, and just hold her while they both got some much-needed shut-eye.

He shook his head. What was he thinking? He could not get involved with this woman. For starters, she was the niece of Sammy the Smoke Byrne. Not to mention, no woman in her right mind would consider a romantic attachment with him after meeting his family. Nor could he support a wife.

She blinked owlishly. "Sorry, I must have dozed off. Is it Creighton? Is he ill?"

He took the hand she'd raised to her chest in worry. "No, he's fine. Sleeping soundly in his room. The aunts are down for their afternoon rest as well."

"Then what?"

She didn't draw her hand away. He blamed the shock of the previous evening and her lack of sleep. But he'd hold it as long as she let him. "I received a telegram. A contact of mine in London who...gathers information about situations that concern me—"

"Your snitch."

He inclined his head. "If you will, although it's usually the coppers that utilize snitches." He wanted to sit, but knew if he moved, she'd remove her hand. "He says that Sam, er, your uncle, has told fellow criminal bigwig Bertie Halprin that he's found the letters and is planning on making his move tomorrow. He's going to hand deliver his demands."

Nick's face blanched. "Oh, no." Now she did pull away. Her eyes took on a distant look, and her mouth grew taut. "I need to go back. I have to get those letters tonight."

"We. We need to go back." Dear God, what was he saying? What was he doing? "I'll help you."

For a moment, something he thought was hope flashed across her face. Then she hardened again. "So you can use them yourself? Set yourself up with a tidy income?"

"No. To help you save your father's reputation and screw Sammy the Smoke out of his prize."

She gazed at him, open-mouthed. No doubt in shock. "You would do that?" Her brow wrinkled. "Why?"

He was an idiot. They'd be carting him off to Bedlam next. But he couldn't deny what he felt, as unexpected as it was. He'd made love to dozens of women and quite a few men in his checkered life. But he'd never felt anything for them. Or nothing like this, anyway. "Because I care about you. More than I should."

She took a step closer. Placed her hand on his chest. His heart thudded against it. "Jack, this is crazy. We don't even know each other."

He placed his own hand over those slender fingers. How had he ever believed she was a young man? He licked lips gone suddenly dry. "I know. But even if you kick me to the curb by Boxing Day, I'm still going to help you."

"I don't know what to say."

He wanted to stay in this moment forever. But the clock was ticking, and the last train to London left in a little more than an hour. "Save it for later. Maybe I'll like your answer better then. In the meantime, we need to get to the train station. Now."

Was she really as reluctant stepping back as he felt like she was? As he wanted her to be? She glanced in the dressing table mirror and made a face. "Good heavens. I look like a charwoman." She reached up and pulled out a handful of pins, and all that pale gold hair came tumbling down. He itched to run his fingers through it.

She snagged the brush from the table, gave the mass a couple of strokes, then bundled it back into a tail. "I'll braid it on the train." She glanced around. "Oh, I'll need my knife." And she grabbed her evening bag and headed for the door.

Just like that. A "grab her knife and go" kind of woman. One who knew how to break into houses like a ghost and, paradoxically, how to dance a minuet. What more could he possibly want?

They spent the trip back to London in worried silence. Once there, they prepared for another nighttime incursion of the house. Jack lent Nick a black jumper, but his trousers were both too long and too big, even with a belt to hold them up. Fortunately, a local men's wear shop Jack used hadn't yet closed, and they found a pair made for a young man that had never picked them up. She had her knife, which they strapped to her hip in a makeshift sheath, and he had a little something in his pocket that, if he got the chance, might do old Sammy the Smoke some damage.

Dressed in overcoats, hats, and gloves, they made their way to Portman Square around midnight. A few lights shone through the windows of Byrne's house, and Nick gave him a rundown. The light in the front of the second story was her father's bedroom, where, as she put it, Sam now 'squatted like a toad'. At the back of the house, no lights shone in the study. Even with the drapes closed, she assured Jack, light leaked out at the top. She'd sneaked in and out often enough, she told him, that she knew the signs.

They slipped around to the rear, and she headed straight for a window near the kitchen door, avoiding the gravel walk. They'd leave prints in the snow—the accumulation fell too light to cover them—but there was no help for it. As they'd discussed on the walk over, they'd either succeed tonight, or they'd fail, and if they failed, what happened after that, at least to Nick, didn't matter. She couldn't see a life beyond that failure.

Jack had other ideas, but he kept his mouth shut.

She pushed up on the window. It didn't budge. Frustrated, she pressed upward again.

In complete silence, he wrapped gentle fingers around her wrist and took her place. Maybe the sash was frozen shut. Careful not to shove too hard—they needed to ease it up as silently as they could—he wiggled it on either side.

Nothing. He mouthed, "Locked."

"Damn it," was her voiceless response. She looked up, then back at the tree they'd shinned down (was it only two nights ago?) and pointed.

He nodded, reached the tree first, thinking to give her a boost, but she jumped up to grab a low-hanging branch and clambered up like a monkey. She carried on, higher than the study window, up to the level of the fourth story, where a rather slender branch reached toward a balcony on a turret that jutted out. He climbed after her, eyeing that thin branch, wondering if it would hold his weight. He wasn't a stalwart sort of fellow, but it would be a chancy thing.

She scooted across the branch and, as it bent slightly, she jumped off onto the tiny spit of a balcony, then motioned for him to join her. Taking a breath and sending up a prayer to Jude, the patron saint of lost causes, he gripped the branch with both hands and scooted forward.

It bowed alarmingly beneath him. But there was nothing to do but continue forward. It was either that or give up, and he wouldn't do that.

When he got within a yard of the balcony, he heard a faint crack. With agonizing care, he got his feet under him as best he could and, before the branch could give way, launched himself toward the railing.

He caught it with one hand, his face banging into the wrought iron as he swung wildly. Nick grabbed his arm to steady him, and he brought his other hand, then his elbow up and over the rail. After a pause to catch his breath and brace his feet, he dragged himself over the parapet.

Nick threw her arms around him, and they stood there for a moment, hearts pounding, chests heaving, both grateful the branch hadn't snapped. Neither of them spoke, and Jack was acutely conscious of how much noise all that scrabbling onto the balcony had made. He was just as keenly aware of her body pressed against him, and as soon as the adrenaline surge passed, he gently put her aside. He pointed at the pair of narrow French doors that led inside. She nodded and mouthed "attic," then stuck the blade of her knife into the leaky gap between the doors and lifted the latch.

The right-hand door opened, and she slipped through the narrow gap into a yawning darkness.

He stood there in the midnight snow, wondering if he'd been a fool, if this was some kind of trap, trying to imagine what awaited him inside.

Then, with a leap of faith, he followed her inside.

Chapter 13

Nicola

The all-encompassing darkness in the attic might have frightened some, but for Nick, it brought back fond memories. The top of the house had once contained a jumble of forgotten treasures. During childhood, it had been her favorite place to play, dressing up in ancient, discarded clothes, dragging crates and trunks around to make cozy hiding places, draped with old tapestries and dusty Turkey carpets. She'd made paths through the mess, creating a maze that the servants had trouble getting through to find her. Except for Creighton, who had always been nimble, and made a game of hunting for her.

A number of months after her father's death, her uncle brought someone in to inventory everything in the house. His "staff", which was now composed of his criminal organization's lackeys, had pawed through the attic, scooting everything to one side or the other of the stairs that led up from the floor below.

Fortunately, she'd gotten her chairs and a few other bits and bobs, like her favorite carpet, before Sam sold everything that was worth the trouble and dumped what wasn't. Now the space lay empty and forlorn, stripped of its purpose. When Jack stepped tentatively through the door—and who could blame him, he had no idea what he was walking into—she took his hand and led him to the stairway, placing his fingers on the banister, so he knew he faced a set of steps.

Although clouds covered the moon, the white blanket of snow over everything made the light coming through the balcony doors seem bright to Nick's dark-accustomed eyes. But even in darkness, she knew her way down the creaky stairs. Jack didn't.

She placed his other hand on her shoulder and led him down, stopping at the door. Pulling his face down to hers, she had to risk a whisper. "Servant's quarters. Left to the stairs, down a floor, then right. Study is third door on the left."

He nodded, his breath tickling her ear. "Thanks."

For a moment, she wondered what would happen if they left right now. Went back to Jack's home, see where whatever spark between them led, and let Sam have the letters. Let her father's peers find out how he'd been cuckolded. Let them know what an idiot he'd been and cast a lurid pall of scandal over everything he'd achieved in his academic life.

Jack squeezed her shoulder and whispered in her ear. "We can do this."

It was like he knew what she was thinking. She reached up, touched his hand in thanks, and after a deep breath, eased open the attic door.

The hallway lay in silence, the kind of silence she'd learned to recognize as a teen, the kind that meant people slumbered deeply, completely unaware of her actions. A peaceful kind of silence.

Nick padded softly down the hall and moved carefully onto the steep, narrow servants' stairs. The door to the floor below had well-oiled hinges—no servant wanted to disturb the members of the household by opening squeaky doors. She opened it a crack, saw the only light burning was the lamp on the table that Creighton used to light at night. Stepping out, she paused, trying to sense her uncle's presence, but the house felt blank. Maybe he was out for the evening again.

Jack moved wraith-like behind her. When they reached the study, she stopped once again, listening with her ear to the door.

More silence.

The hair on the back of her neck stood up. She'd heard nothing. But was it the nothing of someone waiting on the other side? She'd always had a sixth sense about such things, but tonight, that sense felt compromised by the weight attendant upon success. Was this just nerves, or was the room occupied? She hesitated, her hand hovering over the doorknob.

Jack gently nudged her aside again and listened as well. Maybe he had a sixth sense, too. Finally, he looked at her and shrugged.

Screwing up her courage, she pulled her knife from its sheath, and remembering all the horrible things Sam Byrne had done in his life, to her father, to her father's staff, to her, she turned the handle and eased open the door.

Darkness. Quiet.

She moved inside and stepped out of the way so Jack could enter too. Then, in an act of faith, she crept to the mantel and, pulling a long fireplace match from the holder, lit a candle.

Light burst forth like the sun, and she blinked in the brightness. Her gaze flew to the fireplace and the painting of her mother.

And found the space where the portrait had always hung empty.

She ran over. Kicked the empty gilt frame leaning against the bookcase. "Damn him. He really does have them."

"That's where they were? Behind the painting? You must have had heart failure when I was fussing with that, thinking the safe was behind it."

"He's hidden them somewhere else." She glared around her. "Maybe the safe?"

Jack followed her gaze. "Hah. So, it *was* behind the desk. That was my first guess, but I got too clever for myself." Moving behind the mahogany monstrosity, he knelt. "Nick? It's open."

She heard him fumbling around inside it as she crossed the room to join him.

He blew out a frustrated breath. "It's empty. Except for this."

Standing, he handed her a slip of paper that had been folded twice. She opened it and read: You lose.

She looked up at Jack. "That bastard."

The door to the study swung open, and both of them turned at the unmistakable click of a pistol being cocked.

Sam Byrne strode in, holding a gun. Short where his brother had been tall, portly where Arthur was lean, he epitomized what Em's people called nouveau riche. Gauche, tasteless, unmannered, and above all, criminal. "Well, well," he said around an unlit cigar. "Look what got caught in my trap. A wee little mouse trying to sneak back into my larder."

Nick hid her right hand, the one that still held her knife, behind her leg. "Evening, Sam."

"Hello, girlie. Finally decided you've 'ad enough of being a pauper? Slinking home to beg forgiveness? Don't worry. I've got a nice husband all lined up for you. Bertie Halprin and I have a deal, and between the two of us, we'll lock up all the business in this town."

Sam swung the muzzle of the gun toward Jack. "And if it isn't Seamus O'Shea's little brat, all grown up and thinking 'e can play with the big boys. I 'eard you took up your da's trade. Probably hang like 'e did, too.

Nick tore her gaze away from her uncle to look at Jack. O'Shea? Had everything he'd told her been a lie? "What happened to Delacroix?"

His tone was terse, his attention focused on Sam. "My aunts adopted me and legally changed my name."

"I thought your parents died tragically." Wasn't that what Em had said?

His saucy grin had fled, and he clenched his jaw. "Their deaths *were* tragic. Your uncle saw to that. Da strung up for a crime he didn't commit and ma mere dead in a bathtub with her wrists slit over it."

"'E were still a thief. And a bad one at that. Would've hung eventually with or without my interference. I will say it were a damn shame your mum took 'er own life. I coulda found work for a woman like that."

"You're a pig, Byrne." Jack spat at Sam but otherwise remained still. Apparently, Nick wasn't the only one who knew her uncle would enjoy firing that gun.

Sam leered at Nick again. "You've got two choices. You either do the right thing and marry Bernie, or I'll see you're locked up in the nick with this one. Hah, that's a good one. Get it? Nick in the nick?" He chuffed a laugh, then grabbed her left arm. "What's it going to be, girlie?"

She sensed Jack tense. If he rushed Sam, he'd get himself shot, and for more reasons than she could articulate, she wouldn't let that happen. But Sam wanted Nick for his deal with Bertie Halprin. Which meant he would at least pause before shooting her.

Her knife remained clenched in her right hand. Before Jack could do something stupid, she flew at Sam and shoved the knife at his paunch.

Surprised, he twisted and toppled backward, landing hard on the rug. She saw blood, but she'd missed her target, only grazing him in the arm.

The jab and the force of his fall knocked the pistol from his hand, and it slid across the floor, coming to rest against Jack's boot. Sam's fist came up and clocked Nick on the chin, sending her sprawling. By the time Nick scrambled to her feet, Jack stood with his foot on Sam's chest, aiming the gun at Sam.

"Jack, no. Don't let him be the reason you're hanged too."

He didn't look at her, kept his eyes on Sam's now wide baby blues. Before she could react, he flipped the gun in his grasp and whipped the butt into the side of Sam's head.

Sam groaned, then lay still.

"Oh God. Is he...?"

"You're not going to faint on me, are you?" Jack shot her one of his patented grins.

His amused tone relieved her. She didn't believe he'd be that flippant if he'd killed Sam. "Don't be ridiculous. I've never fainted in my life."

"Good. Nice move, by the way. You're fast. And no, he's not dead. But he'll have a helluva headache when he comes to." He tossed the pistol onto the settee. "I hate those things." He grabbed her uncle under the arms. "Come on, now. Help me get him in that desk chair and we'll truss him up. Then we need to find those execrable letters."

She took Sam's feet, and they labored under the man's considerable weight to drag him into the chair and bind him with the tasseled, gold drapery ties.

"I'm sorry about your parents," she said as she stepped back to admire their work—and made sure her uncle's chest still rose and fell.

"And I'm sorry this cretin is your uncle. Is this arranged marriage the reason you took up a life of crime?" He wiped his hands on his trousers, as though just touching Sam made him feel dirty. "And how *did* you learn to burgle like a pro?"

"We need to hurry. No telling when one of his lackeys will come looking for him."

"Fine. We can talk while we look. Come on, spill. You know all of my secrets now."

"Do I?"

"Well. Most of them."

She put her hands on her hips and did a slow turn, taking in the room where she and her father had spent so many happy hours. The blank spot where the painting of her mother had hung mocked her. "It was Creighton's fault."

"Creighton?" Jack, busy rifling the books in the bookcase, sputtered in disbelief. "He's a thief?"

"No. Well, not now. He was, as a boy. He and his three brothers apparently ran in an east end gang. Bos, short for Boswell, is a fence, Wally's a bookmaker, and Charlie is a second story man. On the weekends, when mother wanted to get rid of me, or in the evenings when Father was at his club, I'd be foisted off on the staff. Since Father didn't need Creighton at those times, Creighton would go visit his family, and since there was no one to watch me, he'd take me with." She paused, looking at the mantelpiece. Something was different since she'd last been in this room, and not just the missing painting. "Creighton's real last name is Crichton."

Jack had moved to the desk, scrabbling through and searching under the drawers. Now he looked up. "Wait. Wait just a confounded minute. Your butler is Charlie Crichton's brother?"

"You know Charlie?"

"Nick, anyone who's in my, or rather, our line of work knows Charlie Crichton. He's the best. Or was until he disappeared a half-dozen years ago. Rumor had it he'd done a bunk to the continent after things got too hot for him here."

She jabbed a thumb at her uncle. "That was Sam's doing. Ran him out of town." She did another slow circle, trying to figure out what was different about the room.

"Okay, so you learned from the best. But...why? Why take up stealing?"

She paused, turned to meet his curious gaze. "At first, it was just a lark. Seeing if I could. Little things. Then, as I got a little older, and my friends started having their seasons and, like sheep in the shute, started down the inevitable path of brokered marriages and providing the next heir and a spare, I realized that unless I provided for myself, that was the course my life was destined to take as well."

"You became a thief because you didn't want to get married? "

Men. They simply couldn't understand. "No, that's not it. Maybe, someday, to the right man. But I want the choice to be mine. Not determined by some merging of wealth and titles. Not for the purpose of becoming a mindless accessory who produces children and needlework with equal facility and nothing else." She felt her temper rising and forced down the ire. It wasn't Jack's fault that society was stacked against women.

To her astonishment, he didn't laugh or scoff. Didn't try to talk her out of her opinion. He looked thoughtful, and after a moment, nodded. "Then I'm glad you had a good teacher." And with that, he resumed searching the desk.

Damn, but he kept surprising her. And unlike most men of her acquaintance, in a positive way. With a smile, she too continued her search of the room and, having completed a circle, found herself staring again at the fireplace mantel. "The box!"

At her exclamation, Jack banged his head on the underside of the desk. With a rude word, he crawled out of the kneehole. "What?"

She crossed to the mantel and reached for an 18th-century bronze jewelry box, decorated with two cherubs reaching for each other on the lid, and inlaid hand-painted ceramic scenes on the front, back, and sides. "This belonged to my mother. She claimed it was from Versailles. It wasn't here day before yesterday—it was in the attic. I saw it when I...rescued the chairs for my parlor."

"Hardly looks the sort of thing Sammy the Smoke would store his cigars in."

She snorted. "He's more the ceramic chicken type." She retrieved the heavy thing and held it with trembling hands, frozen by a moment of doubt. If the letters were inside, would Jack take them from her?

He stood watching her. "Open it." His tone was gentle. "They're yours, Nick. I made you a promise and I'll keep it." He smiled, one of the genuine ones that turned her knees to India rubber. "But hurry. We can't stay much longer."

She flipped open the lid of the ornate box. Almost recoiled at the stack of yellowed envelopes inside, tied with a red ribbon. The one on top was addressed to "My Darling Augusta," in florid script.

Nick looked up at Jack, not sure if she felt excitement, nausea, or relief. "They're here."

Chapter 14

Jack

J ack gazed at the letters with a mix of emotions. Relief at finding them, the usual excitement from locating that which he'd come to steal, but also frustration. He'd been so close to that fat payday that could have solved his financial problems. Well, some of them. Now...well, he'd just have to carry on doing what he did best.

He listened for sounds beyond the study as he watched her gazing into the box with a lost look on her face. No one else seemed to stir in the house. Yet. But they needed to get out of here before someone did.

"Nick?"

She looked up. Tears welled in her eyes, and she brushed them away. "What?"

"We need to go. Is there anything else you want from this place? I don't imagine you'll get another crack."

She shook her head and, after removing the stack of letters, set the gilt box back on the mantel.

Something his aunts had once told him about old French jewelry boxes flitted into his head. "Wait. Give me that."

With a shrug, she passed him the heavy cask.

He opened it, felt the bottom through the velvet that lined it. Was there a seam there? Maybe? But there was no time to investigate now. Best just to take it with them, tear it apart at home.

"What are you doing?"

"Sometimes these things have secret compartments, hidden under the lining, either on top or on the bottom."

"For what?"

Jack shrugged. "For whatever seventeenth century ladies wanted to hide, I suppose. We'll bring it, look at it later. Even if there's nothing valuable in it, the aunts will like it. A little reminder of home." He tucked the thing under his arm, then reached into his pocket. "Just one more thing before we go."

"What's that?"

He glanced at Sam, who sat slumped in his chair, still out cold. "We need to do something about him."

Her eyes widened. "Jack, no. He's despicable, but I won't—"

"I'm not proposing we kill him." Did she really think him that awful? "I just want to create a little trouble for him." He pulled out the white handkerchief in which he'd bundled Lady Beatrice's ruby and diamond necklace the night he'd relieved her of it. He'd planned to have an associate dismantle the parure once the theft had faded from memory, then fence the gems, although he'd removed one of the larger rubies for himself. The pieces had been biding time in his own safe at home, wrapped in Lady Bea's monogrammed handkerchief, waiting for the right time.

Uncovering the necklace, he showed it to Nick. "Recognize this?"

She blinked. "Lady Beatrice's necklace."

"And this, I assure you, is *not* paste."

She stared at the fortune in rubies and diamonds for a long moment before flicking her gaze back to him. A slow smile spread across her face. "You mean to implicate Sam in the theft."

He grinned. "I love the way your mind works."

Her smile felt like sunlight. "I like the way yours works, too." She pointed behind her. "Put it in the safe. Then...do we tell the police?"

"We'll have to. Tonight, before he wakes up and finds it there. He'll never be convicted, of course. He has too many judges in his pocket. But it'll cause him some pain, and if we're lucky, a few nights in jail. I know a chap who knows a chap with the ear of the Commissioner. Lady Bea made a huge stink about the jewelry, and the coppers will jump at the chance to get her off their back."

"Didn't Lady Bea suspect you? You were clearly there at the time."

"I cover my tracks well. I spent the weekend in the company of her brother. When she discovered the piece missing next day, I was having breakfast with Thomas in the back garden—who was, I might add, all set to get a quarter of the price after I'd fenced the stones. Since he said I'd been there all night drinking and playing billiards after she and I had our little tryst, and I'd taken pains to see that the necklace wasn't on the premises, I was above suspicion." He couldn't help grinning. "Always good to have friends."

"You are a sneaky man. I like that about you."

Well, thank God for that. She took the bundle, put it in the safe, then paused. After a moment, she stuck the folded slip of paper on top of the handkerchief and swung the safe door shut.

"What did the note say?"

She grinned at him. "You lose."

He took her hand, brought it to his lips, and inclined his head over it. "I bow to the master."

Her eyes sparkled, the grief that he'd seen in them a few minutes before now gone. She inclined her head in a very regal fashion. "As you should." She gave his hand a squeeze before reclaiming hers. "Now we should go."

He headed for the drapes, behind which this whole affair had started, and opened the window. "After you."

Laughing softly, she slipped out into the night.

Chapter 15

Nicola

Jack's aunts and Creighton, bless his heart, had been busy decorating the morning room for Christmas. By the time Nick and Jack arrived, the enormous tree was resplendent with ornaments, candles, and tinsel.

After a meal that could have been served in any great country house, they all retired to the front parlor where Jack played the pianoforte and Nick, at the insistence of Matilde and "granddad" Creighton, led them in singing all the familiar Christmas carols and a few unfamiliar French ones. It felt surreal. And wonderful. Nick didn't want it to end.

When the caroling was done, Creighton gave her a warm hug, something he'd never done before, breaking the decades-old barrier of servant and mistress. She hugged him back tightly and whispered, "Thank you," into his shoulder. "For everything."

"You're very welcome. It's been my pleasure, Miss Nick."

She shook her head. "No. No more Miss. It's just Nick now. And from now on, you're Granddad." Because hadn't he been? All her life and in every way that mattered?

He beamed at her. "If you wish."

He left her to go sit with the aunts, who were arguing over what to wear to midnight Mass. But not arguing like her parents had argued. Just gentle bickering that seemed to be their primary mode of communication. A bickering, she realized, full of love and common experience.

She stood staring into the fireplace, wondering about the future. How to fix up the apartment and replace all their possessions. How to keep her and Creighton safe and warm during the upcoming winter.

How not to miss Jack when they finally parted ways.

"A penny for your thoughts?"

And there he was, at her side, handing her a glass of mulled cider.

She shook her head and took a sip to avoid answering him.

He held out a hand, and with a twinkle in his eye, whispered, "Come with me."

Were he any other man, and she a sensible woman, she would have been suspicious. And would have been a fool to follow him. Instead, she took his hand and let him lead her across to the morning room, now lit only by the candles on the Christmas tree and the fire crackling in the grate.

He took her to the fireplace and pointed. "All ready for delivery of those letters."

"I...I don't have them with me. I left them in my room when I changed for dinner." She smoothed the skirts of the dress Matilde had loaned her.

He grinned. How on earth could a smile turn her knees to aspic? "As it happens, I have them right here."

She took the packet of letters, still tied with the faded scarlet ribbon. None of her father's stuffy academic colleagues had ever known about her mother's infidelity. It would have killed her father, humiliated him, if word had reached the people he admired and worked with. Whatever could be said about her mother, Augusta had at least been circumspect about her affairs. Now, those learned men would never know. Thanks in part to the man standing in front of her.

She gazed up at him, first in gratitude, and then with a narrowing of her eyes. She knew she'd locked her door before coming down for dinner. "Jack, did you break into my room?"

He spread his hands, gave a very Gallic shrug. "Well, I *am* a thief."

She laughed. It felt so good to laugh, felt good even to want to do so. It had been so long. "Yes, you are." A thief of hearts, she thought. She stared down at the envelopes again.

His tone grew sober. "Do you even know what's in them?"

"No. I don't think I want to know."

"If it were me, I'd be dying of curiosity. Then again, that's what usually gets me into trouble."

She met his gaze, thinking she could happily drown in the regard of those cognac-colored eyes. "Did you look? After you stole them from my room?"

He shook his head. "I'm not a complete cad."

"I don't think you're a cad at all, Jack Delacroix. Or O'Shea. Or whatever your name really is."

"Delacroix. Legally, anyway."

"Are you really a comte of something?"

His lips quirked up. "Officially, yes. Although it's a tiny little parcel of land with an abandoned château that will probably collapse into the lake upon which it sits in another ten years. The title is meaningless both here and in France. It does however provide me with a very tiny income, which I turn over to Hugo and Mrs. E so they will keep taking care of the aunts." He waved that away. "Now I have a question for you. How did you know my name?"

She thought back to the previous spring, when she'd had Creighton dig up the name of the man she'd encountered burglarizing Lady Beatrice's house. "I had Creighton ask his brothers about you after the affair at Lady Bea's. I needed to know who I was up against, who my competition was. You were the first other thief I'd encountered."

"Ah. That makes sense."

It hit her then. Creighton had known all along who Jack was. He'd likely have known Jack's father, if only by reputation. His brother Wally, the fence, certainly must have done. Had Creighton been protecting her by not telling her everything? Or worse, been playing matchmaker?

Jack was nodding, as though he could read her thoughts. But instead of replying, he gestured at the packet of letters. "Shall we?"

Did he mean open them? No, because he reached down and set aside the screen in front of the blaze.

With a glance at him, she took a breath. "Rest in peace now, Father." And with a silent prayer, she tossed the letters into the flames.

When they'd been reduced to ashes, and Jack had stirred the fire to make sure nothing remained, he pulled something else from his trouser pocket. Something small, wrapped in a handkerchief, this one with his own initials embroidered in French blue on the corner. "Happy Christmas, Nick."

She raised her hands in protest. "I can't. I have nothing for you."

"Having met you is gift enough. But if you must, then consider this an apology for stealing the march on you with the ruby necklace."

When she balked, he opened up the handkerchief to reveal a one-carat, pear-shaped red gem. "I thought maybe we could turn it into a ring." His voice cracked at the end, and he watched her intently.

She looked at the red stone, then up at him. "Jack..."

He sighed. "Or not. You could always hock it. Keep you and Creighton in tea and biscuits for a while."

Did the gift of the ruby really represent what she thought it did? A sort of proposal? "Jack, we don't even know each other."

He shrugged. "Perhaps I'm a fool, but I know all I need to. I know you're remarkable. I know you're incredibly kind and generous. I know you're wildly intelligent and can make me laugh. I know you can sneak into a house like a ghost. And I know I've never met, nor are likely to meet, another woman like you." He flashed a smile. "I also know you can't carry a tune in a bucket, no matter what your 'grandfather' thinks, and I love you anyway."

She laughed, and when he moved to place the ruby in her hand, she closed his fingers over it. "Let's just see where this takes us, shall we?"

She took a step forward, then another, until she could feel the heat from his body. Saw his eyes widen, his smile soften. Before she could lose her nerve, she rose up and kissed him.

She'd been kissed before but never had it felt like this. His hands slid around her waist, and her arms slipped around his neck, her fingers tangling into those dark, silky curls.

Tittering came from the doorway behind them. Nick felt her cheeks flush with embarrassment when she saw three heads peering around the doorjamb of the morning room. Jack's aunts and Creighton watched them, all grinning broadly. Creighton chuckled, and she heard him say, "Well done, Nick."

Jack strode across the room, and as the three busybodies stepped back, slammed the door shut. When he returned, he swept her into his arms again. "You. God, you. Where were we?"

Nick kissed him again, deeply, hungrily. "You," she breathed, when they next broke apart, "I believe we were seeing where this will take us."

"Mm," he said, as he pressed her closer. "Magical places, I think."

She smiled against his lips. "I'm counting on it."

Epilogue

June 1872

Jack leaned back in his chair on the terrace of Café Gireau and sipped his coffee, watching in pleasant amusement as the waiter made eyes at his wife. Nick remained ignorant of the young Frenchman's attention as she used her broken schoolgirl French to order a couple of pain au chocolat to go with their coffee.

Behind them and far below, the sun sparkled on the deep blue of the Mediterranean, like diamonds on a blue velvet dress.

Nick glanced over at him as the waiter departed. "You're laughing at me."

"I would never." But he grinned.

She kicked him, gently, beneath the table. "Keep that up, you'll be sleeping on a chaise longue by the pool tonight."

He put down his demitasse cup and leaned forward to capture her hand in his, his thumb rubbing the pear-shaped ruby of the ring that adorned her finger. "Wouldn't be the first time in my long and checkered past."

They'd only spent three days in Nice so far, and Jack couldn't recall three more idyllic ones. He thanked whatever saint had told him to take that antique French jewelry box from Nick's uncle's house the night they'd stolen those letters. Inside the box, hidden in a compartment beneath the velvet lining, had been a fortune in emeralds and diamonds. According to Nick's "Uncle Wally", they were seventeenth century and had possibly belonged to someone in the French court of Louis XIII. A collector, Wally assured them, would pay big money for them. And had. Discreetly, of course.

The proceeds had paid for a new roof, a small honeymoon trip to Paris, with a jaunt to show his new bride exactly what her "estate" looked like, and now, over a year later, it had also provided for a nice holiday to the south of France.

Nick gave his hand an affectionate squeeze, but after a moment, her gaze drifted left, fixed on a point above them.

"Still looking at that suite on the 4th floor?"

"I can't help thinking how easy it would be."

He turned to look himself. The suite's owner, a statuesque woman in her fifties, stood at the balcony, posing as if she knew people watched her, hands braced on the rail, her profile elegant against the white-washed wall behind her while an ocean breeze toyed with strands of her dark hair.

"Too much street traffic to climb up. We'd have to come down from the roof."

"Which fortunately is open to guests. There's a garden up there."

"Someone's been doing their research. I thought we were on holiday."

She grinned at him. "We are. But...she's practically advertising. Did you see that sapphire set she wore at dinner last night? The bracelet alone would be enough to re-plumb the kitchen and the upstairs bathrooms."

He laughed and brought her fingers to his lips. "All work and no play makes Jack a dull boy. Besides. We'd need a cat hook."

She scooted her chair closer and turned his face to hers, kissing him. When she whispered in his ear, her caress trailing along his cheek, he shivered. "I brought one."

"You didn't. No wonder your trunk was so heavy." God, what a woman.

She smiled, kissed the tip of his nose. "You can never be too pre-pared."

Not caring about the proprieties, though those were quite a bit looser here than back in stodgy old England, he pulled her close and kissed her properly. "Je t'aime, mon amour."

"Because I travel with a cat hook?"

"Because you're the only woman for me."

"So you agree? From the roof?"

"From the roof. But it better be tonight. There's that party at the embassy and she and that dreadful man she's married to will be attending."

"Won't she wear the sapphires there?"

"No. She'd have something a bit more spectacular for that affair. And, after all, everyone's seen the sapphires already." He marveled at the thrill that crossed her face, at the joy in her eyes. "You'd look lovely in those jewels."

She laughed and tossed some money onto the table. "Wouldn't that be a sight, me wearing sapphire earrings while mucking out the horse stalls at Brandimore House? Come along, darling. Let's go scope out the garden. Then we can spend the afternoon at the beach."

"I cannot believe my wife is making me work on our holiday. If only I'd known what a taskmaster you are, I'd never have married you."

Tucking her arm into his, he squired her out onto the cobbled streets of Nice, looking forward to a little larceny now, and her by his side for the rest of their lives.

Thank You

THANK YOU, Dear Reader!

I hope you loved reading this story as much as I enjoyed writing it! If you did, please consider leaving a review. Reviews not only help the author find new readers but help other readers find books they'll love.

About the Author

Nan Sampson has been creating new worlds and peopling them with quirky characters since she was old enough to hold a crayon. Convinced she was an alien, she spent her adolescence reading SF/F, watching Star Trek, and waiting for her real family to arrive in a spaceship to take her home. Since that didn't happen, she now happily lives through her fiction, where she can time travel, pilot spaceships, cast powerful spells, ride clockwork horses, and find magical macguffins, always finding love along the way. When forced to exist in the mundane modern world, she is an avid history nut, a terrible but earnest gardener, and a consumer of many cups of tea and coffee. She likes to imagine she lives in Roger Zelazny's Amber, but it looks remarkably like the suburbs of Chicago. Who knew?

Sign up for her newsletter for info regarding new releases, fun historical facts, and the occasional scone recipe at www.nansampsonauthor.com

Or chat with her on Facebook: www.facebook.com/nansampson author

Other Books by Nan Sampson

The Coffee & Crime Mysteries

Restless Natives

Office Heretics

Forest Outings

Fringe Benefits

The Magical Underground Series

Your Goyle and Mine

A Djinn and Tonic

That Old Plague of Mine (Coming Soon)

Love and Larceny Historical Romance Novellas

The Christmas Caper

The Valentine's Day Deal (Coming Soon)

The Bonfire Night Plot (Coming Soon)

The New Year's Eve Assignment (Coming Soon)

WITH SUSAN WACHOWSKI
The Harrogate Chronicles Steampunk Adventures

Atahualpa's Mummy

Merlin's Tomb

Aztalan's Idol (Coming Soon)